Published by CRESTON BOOKS, LLC in Berkeley, CALIFORNIA

WWW.CRESTONBOOKS.CO

CIP data for this book is available from the Library of Congress.

Source of Production: WORZALLA BOOKS, Stevens Point, WISCONSIN

Printed and bound in the UNITED STATES OF AMERICA

1 2 3 4 5

WHEELS ~OF~ CHANGE

To my FAMILY

 ~~ PAST AND PRESENT ~~

WHOSE STORIES INSPIRE ME.

~~ D.B.J.

DARLENE BECK JACOBSON
PRESENTS:

WHEELS ~OF~ CHANGE

To Hope, I hope you enjoy Emily's story — love Darlene Beck Jacobson 2016

Chapter 1

Henry's hammer hits iron — ping, pa-ping. Its music feels warm against my chest, like a wool sweater. A blacksmith is a magician. To bend iron like clay and then make it hard again is the best trick.

"Is this carriage really for John Phillip Sousa, the composer of all those peppy marching tunes?" I ask Henry.

"One and the same, Miss Emily."

"Mr. Sousa must want the best carriage he can find," I say.

Henry chuckles. "He'll get that sure enough."

Papa is owner of the Soper Carriage Works and makes the fanciest, most expensive carriages in Washington, DC. I keep an eye out for him, since if he saw me, he would send me home, saying that the barn is no place for a young lady. The truth is, it's the perfect place for me.

I dance across the sawdust-covered floor past Sam,

Papa's woodworker. His saw hums like a busy beehive, slicing planks of wood. I pick up handfuls of the slivers, inhaling their fresh-cut fragrance. The slivers stick to my sweaty palms. I wipe my hands on my dress to shake them off. The slivers stick there as well, like they've found a home. Mama would frown at my soot-and-sawdust gown.

I glide back to the forge, breathing in the sweet wood and varnish smells, and lean on a wooden carriage wheel propped up next to Henry's work area. Even in this soot-covered space, things are neat and tidy, nothing out of place. Papa rents the land, but owns the building and all the equipment inside. Except Henry has his own box of tools that he keeps at the forge. When I ask him why he doesn't use Papa's tools, Henry says, "I've been usin' these familiar ones so long now that they feel like part of my hand."

Pulsing waves of heat make it feel like summer year round. The fire needs to burn red-hot to be the right temperature for bending iron. I stare into the fire's belly, watching it move and change colors as if it were a living thing. Some folks might think the forge is dark and dreary, with only one small window. But the fire is like a beacon that lights up the whole barn and makes it shimmer. Papa's barn without the forge would be like Mama's house without the kitchen. The heart would be gone.

The rhythmic tapping of Henry's hammer is music to me. If I had but one wish, here it is — to be a blacksmith.

"Careful, Miss Emily." Henry wipes soot off his brow with a stained neckerchief. "You lean on that wheel and it slips, you could get hurt."

"May I work the bellows, Henry?"

"You know your daddy don't want you here. Not safe for a young lady."

That's my curse. Being born a girl. Seems like all the interesting things in life are made for boys and men to enjoy.

I sigh.

Henry sips coffee from a tin cup. His chestnut-brown skin is shiny with sweat, but he never complains, even when the heat in the forge could melt a candle. Henry has worked for Papa ever since I can remember. I feel lucky getting to witness his magic every time I come to the barn.

Which isn't often enough to suit me.

Papa rushes past before I can hide, a teetering pile of wood planks on one shoulder, paint cans hung elbow to wrist, like ornaments on a Christmas tree. He stands a head shorter than Henry, but he's strong and solid. His gray eyes don't miss anything.

"Emily, this barn is no place —"

"— For a young lady." I finish the sentence.

"Take those fabric scraps to your mama." He sets the boards and paint cans on the floor and points to a wooden box next to the barn door.

"Papa, can I stay and stir paint?"

"No."

"Sort nuts and bolts? Sweep sawdust?"

"Emily . . . " His grayish-brown mustache twitches in an almost-smile as he nudges me toward the door. Papa is so busy, he hasn't noticed that his hair is mussed and the bald patch on top exposed. He usually combs his hair to cover it. It is the only vain thing I've ever seen him do.

I take one more deep breath and store away the smoky

smell until I can have it again.

I take my time walking back to the house, feeling like I've just been sent to my room without supper. Empty.

The scrap box isn't heavy, just awkward. If I hold it in my arms like a baby, my dress will get dirty. If I set it on the dirt path and kick it most of the way, I'll scuff my shoes. Mama will be less likely to notice scuffed shoes, so I choose that option. By the time I reach the back door, I've not only scuffed my shoes, I've gotten dirt on my stockings and all over the wooden box. I'm really going to suffer Mama's wrath now.

I spit on my shoes and buff them with a scrap of cloth from the box until they look presentable. Brushing off the stockings does no good at all. The more I rub, the darker the stockings get. I wipe off the box as best I can. After picking off the last bits of sawdust from my dress, I give myself a final inspection and say a small prayer that Mama will be too busy to notice anything improper.

"Here's the fabric scraps." I set the box on a chair, hoping Mama won't have her usual sharp eyes.

"Emily Soper, look at you." Mama frowns, hands on hips.

"I'm sorry I messed my clothes, Mama. I'll help you wash and press them, I promise." She doesn't sound too upset with me, so I may get by with just a scolding.

"You are the most unlady-like young lady I've ever laid eyes on." She brushes the sawdust I missed from my hair and shoulders. "If I didn't know better, I'd swear you did these things just to upset me."

If I deny it, it will only give Mama a chance to start naming all those other things. Sometimes it's better to keep quiet. I do my best to look pitiful and sorry.

"Wash up and keep William busy while I finish supper."

At the sound of his name, my four-year-old brother runs into the kitchen, fingers pointing like six-shooters.

"Pow, pow." He blows on his pistol fingers.

"Come out to the watering hole with me, Will. After we wash up, I'll show you how to tie a lasso."

His eyes light up. "Can we ride Colonel and rope some steer?"

"There aren't any cows around here, but we can try it out on the fencepost," I tell him.

"Emily, don't let him get dirty."

"We'll be careful, Mama."

Will grabs an old broomstick Mama uses to poke coal in the stove. He puts it between his legs and says, "Giddy-up," as I follow him out the door.

We rope fencepost steer and lasso imaginary cattle after I do my chores. Thankfully, it's enough to make Mama go easy on me. My punishment ends with washing my dress and stockings — plus a few of Mama's unmentionables — in a tub of soapy water and hanging them in the warm sun to dry.

That means I get to eat supper with the rest of the family.

"The mashed potatoes are a bit lumpy, Ella." Papa reaches for another slice of pot roast.

I like the lumps. They keep my mouth busy while I get all the flavor I can from the gravy before I swallow. I would eat gravy all by itself, but Mama says it isn't proper.

William's face is covered in a potato-gravy mess. He licks gravy off his fingers with no scolding at all.

"When will the carriage be finished?" Mama asks.

"A week from Saturday." Papa looks at me over the top of his glasses. "You going to be ready for a test ride, Emily?"

"Yes!"

Mama shakes her head. "John, don't you think Emily is getting too big for that?"

"Please, Mama!" I yell so forcefully, gravy shoots from my mouth onto the table. Mama frowns, handing me a wet cloth to wipe up the stain.

"You're twelve years old," she says. "Besides, there's a pie-baking contest for children at the church fair the same day. It's about time you learned to bake a good pie. Can't do that from the back of a carriage." Mama scrubs at William's face with a napkin.

"I'll make the pie on Friday," I say. "Then I can still help Papa with the carriage on Saturday. Please, Mama?" I look at Papa, hoping he'll help convince Mama. He's as quiet as snow falling on a moonlit night. I try to wait patiently, but I can't. The snow is just too slow.

"Papa?" I beg.

"What time is the judging, Ella?"

"Two o'clock."

"I can get her home by one."

Mama stares at me for a long minute, as if she's waiting for me to do something I shouldn't.

I put my napkin back on my lap and sit taller in the chair, like a proper young lady.

"You have her here by noon," Mama says.

"Done," Papa says, winking at me across the table.

I slump back down, returning Papa's wink.

"Now, don't you think your mama's pot roast is succulent?"

"What does succulent mean?" I ask. Papa plays this word game nearly every week. He says knowing lots of words helps you in life.

"Succulent means tasty and mouthwatering. Use it in a sentence, Emily."

I think a minute. "Gravy is more succulent than pot roast," I say.

Papa smiles at Mama. "To each his own," he says.

While I'm happy Mama agreed to let me ride with Papa, I sure wish pie baking wasn't part of the deal. Seems like every time I turn around, I have less and less time in the barn. I don't go there just to be idle. I have real work to do. Something Papa knows nothing about.

Chapter 2

Mama has me baking pies all week long. I feel like I've rolled so much dough there's got to be no more flour or lard left in all of Washington, DC. If she didn't let my best friend, Charlie, help, I'd feel like a prisoner baking for the inmates.

I grew up with Charlie. Our mothers have been best friends forever, so it's only natural that we should be too. What makes him different from the rest of the boys at school is that he treats girls like people. He doesn't show off, tease, or annoy us. I guess it's because he's a big brother to four younger sisters and used to having girls around.

Charlie brings in a basket of peaches. "Where do you want these, Mrs. Soper?"

"Set them on the table, dear." She wipes her floury hands on her apron.

Charlie sets the bushel basket down as if it were filled with feathers instead of peaches. Even though he's long and lean like a fencepost, he's strong. He climbs trees faster than anyone and is always hoisting William up onto his shoulders. His straw-colored hair is thick, with so many waves it makes Mama sigh just looking at it. Charlie's hair looks good even when it's mussed — like now.

"Can I take a break, Mama?"

She stares at my blue apron covered with flour. I bet if I spun in a circle, it would seem like a snowstorm had burst into the kitchen.

"You might as well clean up, and you can both have some pie and milk."

"Can I have more, Mama?" William holds up his dish, his mouth covered with pie crumbs.

"You'll spoil your supper," Mama says.

Charlie pokes me in the rib and points to William. "Looks like you have a second helping already, Will. Go look."

William drags a chair over to Papa's shaving mirror, looks at himself, and squeals like a pig in a fresh pile of mud. He licks at crumbs with his tongue and picks off the rest, stuffing them in his mouth.

"William, stop that." Mama wipes his chin with a cloth. "Charles Milton Cook." Mama's eyes flash at Charlie. "Stop encouraging him."

It amazes me how easily Charlie gets along with grown-ups. He's never awkward or unsure of himself. When Mama scolds him, there's a gleam in her eye that's not there when I'm the one being scolded.

Mama cuts us each a slab of pie. My stomach wakes to

the cinnamon-peach smell.

"Is this Emily's?" Charlie asks, sniffing at his piece.

"It is." Mama takes a small slice herself. "We're going to judge it, just like at the contest."

"Oh, Mama. Can't we just eat it?" My stomach is no longer interested in tasting something that might fail Mama's test.

"You can't improve unless you know what needs to be fixed." She lifts a forkful to her mouth, chews, and swallows.

Charlie does the same. His eyes get bigger as he chews. "I like it," he says.

I let out a puff of air I've been holding. "Really?"

He takes another bite. "The peach part is real good."

"It is," Mama says. "But this crust will never do."

"What's wrong with it?" I ask.

"Taste it and tell me," Mama says.

I do. Oh my.

Chewy and starchy, like day-old oatmeal. None of the flakey crispness of Mama's crust. "How did it turn to rubber?" I ask.

"Too much rolling and fussing," Mama says. "Pie crust needs a light touch. The more you work it, the tougher it gets."

I sigh, thinking of Henry's iron. If all that working and hammering is good for iron, it ought to be good for pie crust. Charlie lifts up a chunk of crust with his fork. "I bet it would hold up pretty good at the shooting range."

I stick my tongue out at him.

"Now, Charlie," Mama says, smiling.

"I hope you two are enjoying yourselves," I say, thinking how much better it would be if I could enter a carriage-making contest. I eat the last of the peach filling, wondering if I'll ever be able to live up to Mama's proper standards.

Taking out his special magnifying glass, Papa gives the carriage a final inspection on Saturday morning. He stares at one spot so long, I wonder if we'll ever leave. He runs his fingers over the spot. Sam, the woodworker who cuts out carriage pieces and does upholstery, gives it his own inspection one more time before Papa nods. Finally, I climb onto the seat beside Papa. He slaps the reins at our horse, Colonel, and we're off to deliver the finished carriage.

"What do you think of this one, Emily?" Papa asks as we travel the bumpy dirt-and-cobblestone roads through the district.

"She's a beauty." I run my hand over the plaid wool seat. "All your carriages are works of art."

"A few places didn't come out quite as I'd hoped."

"Papa, you always say that. And every time I look over each new carriage, I never see even a tiny mistake."

Papa smiles the crinkle-eyed smile I love and sighs. "When you do something, it can be with pride or indifference. Always aim for pride."

"You can be proud of this one," I tell him.

Papa stops the carriage at Seventh Street. With shops, businesses, and factories, it's one of the busiest streets in DC. Mama swears by the goods in Kahn's Department Store. They have reasonable prices, and if you aren't satisfied with a purchase, you can return it. She also likes to wander around in Grogan's Furniture Store, though she never buys anything.

I can hardly stand to spend a few minutes in either place. I suspect it's more of a proper-lady type experience.

I prefer to spend my browsing time at Center Market across the street. All the fresh fruits, vegetables, and other tempting stalls seem to go on forever. So much food under one roof is amazing to behold. My mouth waters every time I get near there.

"Take a look at that," Papa says, nodding toward the street teeming with cable cars, wagons, and carriages.

"Oh my . . ." I catch my breath at the sight of what looks like a carriage whizzing by. It's sleek and shiny, but there's no horse pulling it. It groans, sputters, and spews out a gray cloud of awful-smelling smoke as it passes. The driver wears goggles that cover half his face while his passenger wears a scarf that flutters in the breeze like a flag.

"What kind of a carriage is that?" I try to hold my breath until the foul smell passes.

"It's an Oldsmobile motorcar," says Papa.

"Where's the horse?" I ask. I don't know whether to be amazed, scared, or upset at such a sight.

"It has an engine and doesn't need one. Some run on steam, others on gasoline."

"Do they make them in a carriage barn, like you do, Papa? How do you start and stop it? How does it turn?"

Papa sighs. "They're made in big factories, Emily. They have a special wheel for steering and a pedal you step on to stop the car."

"It sounds like something out of a dream. Like make-believe."

"It's real, all right." He shakes his head, frowning.

"The world is changing too fast for me."

"Is change a bad thing?"

"Some folks welcome it. Others —" Papa taps Colonel, and the carriage moves again.

"Others what, Papa?"

"Others get used to life being a certain way and are content with that."

"I like things the way they are," I say.

"Me too, Emily."

"Can't folks decide for themselves whether to change or stay the same?"

I wonder if Papa heard me since he doesn't answer right away. Finally, he says, "Some change you can brush away like dust and it won't bother you at all. Other change comes at you like a flood and sweeps away everything you know, leaving strangeness behind."

"The world can change as much as it wants," I say. "I just won't pay any attention to it, as long as I get to ride in your carriages and watch Henry make magic in the barn."

"Amen to that," Papa says.

We ride the rest of the trip in silence, enjoying the warm sunshine, the farms and businesses we pass, and being together. As much as I thrill to each new carriage ride, the best part is spending time with Papa. I let Mama think it's all about the carriage so as not to offend her. Is it a sin to like one parent over another? I hope not, because there's nothing I can do about it.

Chapter 3

After we drop off the carriage, Papa and I ride back on Colonel and arrive home as Mama and William are packing our pies for the church fair. Mama made her own peach pie for the contest. There will be prizes for the ladies as well as for the girls.

Mama looks me over. I know she'll make me change if something isn't right. I examine my dress. It's nearly as clean as when I put it on.

"We don't have much time," Mama says. "Wash up and fix that wild hair."

I sigh and do as she asks. I just want to get this part of the day over with.

"Guard these pies with care," Mama says. I set the basket on my lap, lifting the cloth that covers our pies. By smell alone, these pies are winners. William sits next to me in our open phaeton carriage while Mama sits in front with Papa.

When we get to the church, it seems like every wagon and carriage in town is here, a few of them made by Papa.

"You better get off here," Papa says. He helps Mama down. I hand the precious pie basket to Mama and hop off, dragging William behind me. We follow Mama through a crowd of people to the pie tent.

I spot Charlie flying out of the tent so fast, you would think he was trying to escape from a bear.

"Why are you in such a hurry?" I ask.

He flicks a thumb toward the tent. "Bea Pea is in there."

"Thanks for the warning." An unexpected visit from a bear would be more welcome than one from Beatrice Peabody. Better known as Beatrice Busybody or Bea Pea, as Charlie likes to call her. If boasting and gossip were subjects in school, Beatrice would be the star pupil. She spreads rumors like a mosquito spreads malaria. Although, if I cared for girl things, I'd want hair like Beatrice's. The same chestnut brown as Henry's skin, with lots of curls and shine. My hair is wispy and stands out in every direction like the quills of a scared porcupine.

"Mama, do I need to stay in the tent now?" I hand William over to her.

"Help me set the pies down, and then you and Charlie can walk around a bit."

Mama finds an open spot at the ladies' table for her pie.

"Good afternoon, Martha." Mama smiles at the lady behind the table.

Old Mrs. Crabtree — perfectly named to fit her

grouchy disposition — nods her greeting to Mama and gives the rest of us the once-over. Her freckled forehead is so full of frown wrinkles, it reminds me of a freshly plowed field. She never smiles. Mama says it's because she's had a hard life caring for nine children — including one with a lame leg — and a husband who's a merchant seaman and gone most of the time.

With a life like that, it seems like you'd welcome an opportunity for a laugh now and then.

"Are you entering pies this year, Martha?" Mama asks.

"Waste of time with you and Mrs. Peabody being such good bakers. I put my sour pickles up for judging."

Charlie pokes me in the rib with his elbow. We're thinking the same thing — if Mrs. Crabtree's pickles match her expression, she's a blue-ribbon winner for sure.

We sign our names on a sheet of paper, and Mrs. Crabtree gives us each a number. Mama's is ten. Ten fingers, ten toes, Ten Commandments. That seems like a lucky number for any contest.

I'm stuck with six. I can't associate it with anything important. Half a dozen, half the months of the year. A pie half as good as all the others. I sigh and follow Mama to the girls' table.

"Good afternoon, Mrs. Soper, Charles and Emily." Beatrice greets us at the table in a voice so syrupy, it makes my teeth ache.

"Hello, Beatrice," Mama says. "Where's your mother?"

"She's judging the jam."

"Isn't she entering her pies this year?"

"Of course," Beatrice gushes. "It wouldn't be a contest if she didn't."

Mama looks up toward the tent ceiling, as if she's hoping for Divine Intervention. Mrs. Peabody's pies always win. "Do you have a pie in the contest?" Mama asks.

"I have two," Beatrice says. "I couldn't decide on peach or apple. They're both my best, so I made one of each. Numbers four and five. What did you make, Emily?"

If Mama weren't standing next to me, I'd tell Beatrice it's none of her business what kind of pie I made. I put my number-six pie next to her number five and say, "Humble pie. You've probably never heard of it."

Bea Pea presses her lips together to keep any nonsense from falling out of her mouth in front of Mama.

"Do you have a pie too, Charles?" Beatrice laughs as if this is the funniest thing anyone has ever said.

Charlie winks at me. "I'm one of the judges."

That shuts Beatrice up. When she realizes Charlie is joking, she puffs and sputters as if someone's let the air out of her.

"Stay tidy, Emily," Mama warns. "Be back here before the judging." She gives me a penny. "Buy some peanuts if you get hungry."

After Mama leaves, Beatrice tosses her hair and says, "I knew you weren't clever enough to make anything but trouble, Charles Cook."

"What do you know, Beatrice? Charlie could make a pie if he wanted to. And who cares about pies, anyway?"

"You won't be a proper homemaker if you can't bake a good pie." She looks at me as if I'm wearing a dunce cap.

"Says who?" I am this close to throwing my number six at her smug, shiny curls.

"Well, I happen to know for a fact . . ."

When Beatrice says that, you know it will be followed by something fantastic, unbelievable, and most likely untrue.

I feel my face getting hotter by the minute.

Charlie takes my arm and leads me out of the tent.

"Don't get upset because of Bea Pea," Charlie says. "Or should I say H. P.?"

"H. P.?" I ask.

He grins. "Humble Pea."

"Grumble Pea, Mumble Pea." I say.

"Stumble Pea." Charlie laughs. "Let's forget about her and look at the baby pigs. Their squeals are easier on the ears." He digs into his pocket. "I have a penny for some licorice sticks."

"And I have one for peanuts."

We stop by a canopy where Charlie's father has his prize watermelons. I smile at Holly, Charlie's eight-year-old sister. She's grins at me with a slice of watermelon in her mouth so she looks like a clown. I poke Charlie in the ribs and we both laugh.

"Hi there, Emily," Mr. Cook says. His rust-colored beard shines in the afternoon sun. "Did you hear Rose's good news? She and Mrs. Cook got second prize for their jam."

"No fooling?" Charlie says.

"That's splendid," I say. Rose is ten and my favorite of all of Charlie's sisters. Besides Rose and Holly, there is Iris who's four and Daisy who's three. "Where is Rose now?"

"Last I heard, they were going to the quilt barn to look at all the fancy quilts. Probably still there, I reckon," Mr. Cook says.

Charlie and I look at each other, silently deciding

that's the last place we want to be.

"Have a nice piece of watermelon. It's quite refreshing on a day like today." He cuts two large wedges and hands them to us.

We step into the sunshine to enjoy the treat. I take a bite with juice dribbling down my chin. Mr. Cook was right about it being refreshing. Charlie grins and spits a watermelon seed. It lands on the lacy edge of my dress sleeve, stuck like a beetle in a spider's web. I grin back at him and take another juicy bite, working the melon around my tongue until I capture the seed, take aim, and spit.

My first try falls pitifully short of Charlie, landing on his shoe. Fortunately, the watermelon is full of sticky black seeds, so I get a lot of practice. By the time I'm finished eating, I've landed a fair amount of seeds on Charlie's shirt and trousers.

"I think I did pretty good," I say, tossing the rind in a trash barrel.

"Not as good as I did." Charlie laughs.

When I look down at my dress, it's covered in black polka dots. I spin around and shake, trying to loosen them. Not a one budges. I flick off a few, but the warm sun has baked them onto the cotton, so it takes more than a flick to get them off. Just when I think I've picked off the last one, I find another.

"Mama is not going to be pleased."

"We can worry about that later," Charlie says. "Let's feed the baby goats. I've got a pocketful of grass."

We have a grand time feeding the kids. Being outdoors with animals is one of the things I like most when I'm with Charlie. Some of the best times we've had have been exploring the woods around our neighborhood. Charlie knows tons about insects and the animals that make the woods their home. One time, we poked a burrow with a stick and got surprised by a skunk. Our mamas wouldn't let us into our houses until we'd washed and scrubbed the stench away. I scrubbed until my skin was raw and pink and I still smelled like skunk. Mrs. Cook made Charlie sleep in the barn. "As long as you stink like that, you may as well be with the rest of the smelly things," she'd said. I had to sleep on a blanket in the carriage barn, which wasn't punishment at all. But I didn't tell Mama that.

We get so involved enjoying the animals, we nearly miss the contest. We run back as fast as we can. After all the work making my pie, I sure don't want to make Mama upset by being late for the judging.

CHAPTER 4

"I was beginning to wonder where you were," Mama says as Charlie and I shove our way to the front of the crowd.

"Sorry, Mama. We were enjoying the farm animals so much we forgot about the time. Did we miss anything?"

"The judging for the ladies' pies is about to start," Mrs. Cook says. Rose and Holly are next to her. Rose has a red ribbon pinned to her dress.

"Congratulations on your prize," I say. "What kind of jam was it?"

"Wild blackberry." Rose's face lights up with a smile that brings out the dimples in her cheeks. "It's my first ribbon."

She isn't boasting like Beatrice would, so it's easy to feel happy for her.

"Do you have a pie in the contest?" Rose asks.

"Yes. Mama too."

"We didn't do pies this year because Charlie —"

"Oh, Rose," Charlie says, "did you see the baby goats?" He gives Rose a funny look that makes her blush and cover her mouth with her hand. Like she was about to say something she shouldn't.

"Hush," Mama says. "The judging is about to begin."

The Reverend and Mrs. Porter are the judges, same as always. Anyone can tell they really like pies. Their bellies are round and cheeks peach-colored from every bite. If you could get paid for eating pies, I bet they'd earn a good living.

Charlie hoists William onto his shoulders so he can see above the crowd. The spectators quiet down as the Reverend and Mrs. Porter sample each pie. They scribble on a paper, whisper back and forth, and sip water between each bite. When they're done, Mrs. Peabody wins first place, Mama wins second, and someone I don't know wins third.

"Number ten was such a good number, I thought for sure you'd be first," I say.

"Yay, Mama," says William.

"If I was judging, Mrs. Soper, I'd have given you first," Charlie tells Mama.

"Me too," says Rose.

Mama smiles. "That's kind of you to say, children. But you know how hard it is to beat Mrs. Peabody. She's been winning for years."

Mama looks at her red ribbon with a gleam in her eye, so I can tell she's plenty satisfied placing second.

Even with so many folks gathered around, it's easy to spot Mrs. Peabody. She's the most colorful, loud, and sizable object in the tent. People are congratulating her as if she's just been made Queen of the Capitol. Face pink with pride and silk fan flapping, she's enjoying every minute of the attention.

Everyone moves to the children's table as the judging starts all over. There are only twelve pies, so it doesn't take long. The Reverend and Mrs. Porter aren't supposed to know who baked each one. The ladies kept quiet when it was their turn, but now as each pie is tasted, a girl fidgets, blushes, and giggles, so only a blind and deaf person would not know the baker of each pie. Except for the number-two pie. I can't figure out who the baker of that one is.

When my pie is tasted, I hold my breath and cross my fingers, no tittering for me. At least the Reverend and Mrs. Porter don't gag on it. I don't expect to win first or second, but maybe third? That should be good enough to please Mama.

The Reverend and Mrs. Porter whisper and pass notes back and forth. They look at each other and smile. Reverend Porter speaks.

"We have the winners. Third place is —"

My heart skips a beat as Reverend Porter looks at the paper.

"— number twelve, the blackberry pie."

I feel like the wind's been knocked out of me. It's a girl I don't know. Her family congratulates her, and she blushes when the Reverend hands her the white ribbon.

"Second place is number five, the apple pie."

Hands clap as Bea Pea holds up her number and beams at the judges. I guess she figures she has first place as well.

I'm afraid to look at Mama. I guess I could have taken it easier on the crust. Why can't I be the kind of daughter she wants me to be? Shouldn't I be able to hammer iron and bake pies?

"The first place winner is number two, the peach pie."

All the color drains from Beatrice's face. So it isn't her pie after all. Number two is the mystery pie, the one nobody giggled or fidgeted over.

This time applause is followed by whispers of "Whose is it?" and "Who baked the pie?" Just when it seems that no one will claim the blue ribbon, Charlie lifts Will off his shoulders and takes a piece of paper from his trouser pocket. He hands it to the Reverend.

"Are you number two, my boy?"

Charlie nods, a smile spreading across his face.

"Charlie," I say, "you didn't tell me you entered the contest!"

"That's why I didn't do a pie," Rose says. "We didn't want to go against each other."

"When I watched you do it, I thought I'd give it a try." Charlie grins. "I didn't think I'd win."

I am so pleased, I want to dance on the tables. Charlie's win is the best surprise. I don't care about losing anymore, now that my best friend beat Beatrice.

"Excuse me," Beatrice's shouts. Once she has everyone's attention, she says, "How can a boy win when the contest is for girls?"

There is muttering and whispering from the crowd. Girls' heads bob up and down and all eyes are on the Reverend. "Well now, it is highly unusual to have a boy enter the contest."

"It never happened before!" someone shouts.

The Reverend clears his throat.

"The contest has always been for girls," Beatrice says. "It's not fair to change the rules at the last minute."

Beatrice rushes over to her mother and says something I can't hear.

Mrs. Peabody dismisses her court of worshippers and waddles to the judges' table, settling her plumage right in front of the Reverend and Mrs. Porter.

"See here, Reverend. There has been an error." She flaps her fan for emphasis.

"Whatever do you mean, Mrs. Peabody?" Beads of sweat line his forehead like pearls on a necklace.

"Did you or did you not award my peach pie first place just a few moments ago?" She flaps her fan at the blue ribbon pinned on her sleeve.

"Yes." The Reverend clears his throat again.

"Then you must have made a mistake by not choosing Beatrice's peach pie for first place as well. I had the peaches shipped from my sister's plantation in Georgia, so I know they are the best quality. I also know my Beatrice used the same peaches in her pie. So therefore, her pie should win first place as well."

Reverend Porter pulls at his collar, blows out a puff of air, and says, "We've already chosen the winner."

"A boy?" Mrs. Peabody looks at Charlie as if he were something on the bottom of her shoe. "When in the history of this contest has a boy ever entered?"

"It is unusual, but — we — " Reverend Porter wipes his brow and stares at the ground.

Mrs. Peabody turns toward the crowd and bellows, "Surely I'm not the only one who finds this whole thing ridiculous. We can't have a boy winning the contest."

"Why not?" I shout.

"Emily." Mama puts a hand on my shoulder and gives me a look that means I am to be seen and not heard.

I listen to the yelling back and forth of the spectators' opinions on the subject. Then I look at the sign hanging above the table. There it is in black and white.

Once the commotion has died down a bit, I say, "Pardon me, Reverend Porter, sir, the sign over your head says it's a children's pie contest. It doesn't mention boys or girls."

There's a hush as everyone reads the sign.

Reverend Porter wipes his brow again and smiles. "Miss Soper is correct. So here you go, young fellow." He hands the blue ribbon to Charlie.

"You haven't heard the last of this. I intend to register a formal complaint." Mrs. Peabody stares at me so long, I feel a chill travel down my spine.

I refuse to look away. When Mama turns to leave, I stick my tongue out at Mrs. Peabody and Beatrice until they both turn their noses up in the air and flounce out of the tent.

They could learn a thing or two from Mama about being satisfied even when you don't get first place. Mama's a winner even without any ribbons, while no amount of prizes can improve on Bea Pea.

At supper, I tell Papa about Charlie's win.

"Mrs. Peabody was not happy," I add.

"I was surprised to see her behave so rudely," Mama admits.

"That shouldn't surprise you, Ella. Mrs. Peabody is strong willed and can be quite —" Papa clears his throat and continues."Opinionated."

"She does like to make her views known," Mama says. "Not that I approve of any such thing, mind you." She looks at me when she says this.

"Of course not, Mama." I want her to know that I don't like Mrs. Peabody's behavior either.

"I always found Charlie to be proficient, but I never guessed his skills included pie making," Papa says.

"Is proficient good?" I ask.

"Better than good. Highly competent."

"I am not proficient at pies and other girlish things," I say. "I'm sorry my pie didn't win a prize, Mama."

"There's a lot more to being a girl than pies," Mama says. "I was pleased at how you noticed the sign while the rest of us didn't. It was good thinking for anybody, boy or girl."

Mama's praise feels like warm honey on a sore throat. How wonderful it would be to have a spoonful every day.

"However, I wasn't pleased with the change I saw in your good cotton dress."

My face flushes. I'd forgotten about the watermelon seeds.

"How on earth did you manage to get all those seeds stuck on your dress?" Mama and Papa are both looking at me, but I see a smile twitching at the corners of Papa's mouth.

I explain about the spitting contest as William's eyes get bigger.

Mama just shakes her head. She scolds William for spitting a pea at me across the table. "See what you've started," she tells me.

Papa is really smiling now, but he is hiding it behind his napkin.

"Don't think you're done with girlish things, as you call them. I'm determined to make a proper lady out of you yet," Mama says.

"If anybody can do it, you can, Ella," Papa says, all serious again.

I sigh. No matter how messy my dresses or how bad my pie crusts, I know Mama will keep on trying.

CHAPTER 5

Since school started, I don't get to spend much time in the carriage barn. As sixth graders, Charlie and I don't often play in the schoolyard anymore, either. Miss Carlisle, our teacher, has us older students helping the younger ones. That means whatever work I don't finish, I have to do during recess or after school. I try not to give up my after-school time. What I do then is my business.

After a week of arithmetic problems, grammar lessons, and chores, I am finally free to work on my important project. I'm making a miniature carriage for Papa. I haven't told Mama or even Charlie. Sam and Henry know because they helped me get started. I got the idea from Henry after he made a small wagon for his daughter to put her dolls in.

Sam let me trace the pattern I made onto some scrap wood. I wanted to cut it out myself, but he wouldn't let me. "I won't risk anything happening to you," Sam said, "even if it is for your daddy." So I had to settle for watching. At least I get to sand and paint the wood.

Henry is helping me with the iron frame and wheels. Again, I asked to do my own forging, but Henry wouldn't let me near the fire, so we worked out a satisfying compromise. On a small anvil away from the heat, I get to bang the iron three times before Henry takes it to his anvil to complete the shape.

I haven't had a chance to work on any part of it for weeks, since I have to wait until my chores are done and Papa isn't around.

"How you been, Miss Emily?" Henry asks as I bring him a pitcher of fresh water from the sink pump. He pours some into his cup and takes a long sip. "That's mighty refreshin' in this heat." He wipes his forehead with a sooty rag.

"It's been forever since I've been in here," I say. "How are things going on you know what?" I glance around to make sure Papa isn't in view.

He chuckles, and his eyes crinkle up in a pleasing way that reminds me of Papa.

"Did a good bit of the frame when you and your daddy were deliverin' the carriage to Mr. Sousa," Henry says.

"That's grand," I say. "I sanded all the wood pieces. Do you think we can work on the wheels today?"

Henry rests a hot rod of iron on the anvil and says, "Your daddy's been in and out all day. If you want to keep this a secret, we best wait for another opportunity." He hammers the rod seven times before putting it into the fire.

"Then maybe I can nail the wood pieces together. I'll

check with Sam."

But Sam is just as discouraging. "I expect your daddy to be back any minute now. He's meeting with a new customer." He takes out his pocket watch. "Said he'd be back around noon."

I trudge back to Henry, kicking soot and sawdust with my shoe. "How am I going to finish the carriage in time for Christmas if I can only work when Papa's not here? Isn't there a place I can work where Papa won't see me?"

Henry stops hammering and stares at me like he's thinking.

"You could do some hammerin' — if you're careful — back behind the barn. Your daddy hardly ever goes back there."

Henry sure gives my spirit a lift with that suggestion.

We load all the wood pieces, nails, and a small hammer into a pail, and I follow Henry around the back of the barn. We set boards across a couple of sawhorses for a worktable.

"If I had a piece of canvas, I could hide my work underneath," I say.

"Good idea," Henry says.

The best thing about this location is that I have a perfect view of the road leading to the barn so I can see when Papa is on his way back.

I slide the wooden seat and back pieces into the slots Sam cut on the carriage sides. Just when I've finished hammering everything in place, I spot a wagon coming up the path. I stash the hammer and nails in the pail under the canvas and run back into the barn well ahead of Papa.

I tuck the model under another piece of canvas Henry gave me, and we set it in the forge. Papa never goes through

31

Henry's things, so it's safe.

"Do you need any help?" I ask. I know I should leave, that I'm not supposed to be here, but I can't help it. I just want a little more time in my favorite place.

"You could fill that bucket," Henry says.

I fill the nearly empty bucket with water from the pump outside. I set it next to the rail of the forge. Papa always wants water close by. Just in case. Maybe if he sees how useful I am, he'll figure it's fine for me to be here after all.

Henry smiles. "I don't know how many horseshoes I'll be needin' to make. Think you can count the horseshoes in this box?"

"Sure, Henry." That's another way to be useful that's not dangerous at all.

Henry lifts up the heavy wooden box filled with horse-shoes and sets it next to me. There are loads of these wooden boxes all over the barn. What makes this one special is the imprint of a horseshoe branded onto one side.

I look into the box. "Henry, why are there so many different sizes?"

"Well now, Miss Emily, do you and your daddy wear the same size shoe?"

I laugh. "Of course not."

"Well, it ain't no different with horses. Some have big feet and some little, just like folks."

"I guess it was a silly question. I should have figured that out myself."

"No question is silly when you're learning about things." He sets the box down on the dirt floor, and I start my sorting and counting.

It only takes a minute to count them. I sort them by size before putting them back in the box, so I can watch Henry work his magic.

Some folks don't like that Papa has a colored man working for him. They think white folks should leave colored folks to work with their own kind. It makes me sad to think that some people can make an important decision about who might be a good worker or a good person just by what color skin he has.

Papa hired Henry because he's the best blacksmith in the whole of Washington, DC. Papa said, 'If I am making a fine carriage, why wouldn't I want a fine worker like Henry?'

When I'm feeling my meanest, I sometimes wish all the people who judged folks by their skin color were struck blind. Then would it matter? Papa says if I wish for things like that, then I'm no better than the people I'm wishing it on.

Still, I can't help wishing it.

"How many horseshoes you count?"

"Forty-five."

"What am I going to do with an odd number of shoes?" Henry shakes his head. "You're just going to have to take one."

"Really?" I feel like it's my birthday and I've just been given the best present. I go through the box until I find the one meant for me. I know it's the one I should take because when I hold it in my hand, it feels warm. Like it's found a home.

"That the one you want?"

"Yes."

"You rub it with this here wire brush and it'll come up nice and shiny."

I do as he says and am pleased to almost see myself in the polished iron.

"Now, when you hang it on your wall," Henry says, "make sure it points up."

"Why?"

"So your luck doesn't run out."

I press the horseshoe to my cheek, feeling pretty lucky already.

"Did everything work out with you know what?" Henry asks, winking.

I nod. Sharing such a special secret with Henry makes me feel like I'm his apprentice and we're working side by side.

"You better run on home," Henry says. "Seems to me you've stretched your time out here as far as it can go."

"Thanks for the horseshoe, Henry."

I nearly knock over Papa coming in with bottles of glue. "You aren't bothering Sam or Henry, are you?" Papa asks. "I don't know how many times I've told you, this is no place for a young lady."

My face gets warm even though I haven't done anything I should feel guilty about. Isn't it funny that even good secrets can make your heart beat faster?

"I was only here for a little while," I say, which isn't exactly a lie, because really, it wasn't very long at all, not nearly as long as I wanted. "Henry gave me a horseshoe that I'm going to hang on the wall over my bed."

"Check with your mama before you make any holes in the wall."

I stop behind the barn to retrieve the hammer and nails before I head home, my heart heavy with keeping secrets.

The house smells like onions. Mama's poking through the icebox, pulling out a leftover piece of ham, two wrinkled carrots, a parsnip, and some lima beans. It's Friday, so I know we're having leftover soup. Mama piles the ingredients in a big bowl and sets it in the sink. William is playing with potato skins, lining them up on the table and poking holes in them with a fork.

"Now that you're here," Mama says, "you can peel and cut these vegetables for the soup." She hands me a pail, shaking her head. "While you're at it, wash the soot off your face and hands. How do you always manage to get so dirty?"

"Henry gave me this horseshoe, Mama." I rest it on the table, hiding the hammer in the folds of my dress.

"What do you plan to do with it?"

"May I please hang it in my room?" I figure if I ask as nicely as I can, it will be harder for her to say no. "Henry says it brings you luck when you hang it pointing up."

Mama stops chopping and stares at me, her face softer, eyes sparkling. "My daddy had one hanging in the kitchen above the door. He said that way luck would be with you coming and going."

I like it when Mama tells stories about my grandparents. I never got to meet them, so the stories help me figure things out about them. One of my favorite stories is how my grandma and her daddy used to hide runaway slaves in a place called the Underground Railroad. When I first heard it, I asked Mama how they built the trains underground. She laughed and told me it had nothing to do with real trains, but everything to do with safe passage to freedom.

"Can we hang this one over the door to remember

Grandpa?"

"I like that idea. After you chop the vegetables, you can ask Papa for a hammer and nails."

"I already got them." I bring the hammer out from its hiding place.

"Then set them aside until Papa gets home." Mama still has the hint of a smile on her face, so I decide to be bold.

"I'd like to hang up the horseshoe myself."

"Oh you would, would you? I suppose it's foolish of me to ask where you learned to use a hammer."

My face reddens again, but I keep quiet, figuring it's less likely to cause me trouble.

Mama stares at me, the hammer, and then the horseshoe. Will watches us both as if we are suddenly much more interesting than potato peels.

Finally, Mama says, "Hang it on the molding above the door. The wood there is softer than plaster and easier to hammer."

"How do you know that?"

"It just so happens that I was the one who hung the horseshoe over our own door," Mama confesses.

It's my turn to stare at Mama. I can't help but wonder if there are other unladylike things she can do.

As if Mama read my mind, she says, "While it may not seem to be a proper skill for a woman, I think it's useful for everyone to know how to hammer a nail. To hang a picture or mirror doesn't require a man's brute strength."

An idea sparks in my head like a match catching fire.

"Let's hang it together," I say. "I'll do one nail and you do the other."

Mama picks up the horseshoe. I slide the kitchen chair in front of the door and hand her the hammer and a nail. Stepping onto the chair, Mama settles the nail into the left end of the horseshoe and pounds the nail as if she's done so all her life.

I take my turn and do the same with the other end.

We stand back to look at it. I like the sparkle in Mama's eye, especially since I am the one who put it there.

"What do you think, William?" Mama asks.

I lift him onto the chair so he can have a better look.

"Giddyup," he says. "I have to pee."

Mama and I laugh. I take William out to the privy feeling full of the horseshoe luck. When a monarch butterfly rests quietly, perfectly, on the outhouse door, it's as if the rest of the world is sharing some of that luck.

Chapter 6

"Well, I happen to know for a fact that it's only a matter of time until everyone owns a horseless carriage," Beatrice says at recess.

She's talking about a small wooden toy Charlie brought to school. A miniature horseless carriage. Charlie and some of the other boys have been passing it around all day.

"You don't know what you're talking about," I say. "I don't know anybody who owns one." I look at Rose. "Do you?"

She shakes her head.

"My uncle George works for Mr. Ford in Michigan," Beatrice says. "Right now only rich people have automobiles. But Father says that because of Mr. Ford's modern assembly-line production methods, the price will come down, and soon everyone will be able to afford one." Beatrice has a look on her face like a buzzard who has just dined on a fresh kill.

"Maybe as a toy," I say. I take the tiny automobile from Charlie, turning it over in my hands. Except for the front where Charlie says the engine would be, it doesn't look much different than a carriage. Is it possible it can move without a horse pulling it? Why would someone even want that?

"I think it's ridiculous. What do you think, Rose?"

"It might be fun to ride in one. Charlie says they're fast as lightning."

I hand the toy back to Charlie. "Really, Charlie?"

"You can go thirty-five miles an hour in one of these things." He's wide-eyed at the thought of so much speed.

"You can gallop pretty fast on a horse," I say.

"A horse needs to rest and be fed. And be cleaned up after. You get in one of these things, crank it up, and go." Charlie's rubbing his hands along the toy like it was Aladdin's magic lamp. I've never seen him so excited.

"It's a modern miracle," he adds.

"Then, what's going to happen to carriages?" I suddenly feel cold, like my body is covered in snow.

"It's going to make carriages obsolete," Beatrice says, all smug and satisfied.

I think back to the day Papa and I delivered Mr. Sousa's carriage and we saw an automobile zip down the road. It didn't bother me too much then. One automobile on a street filled with carriages and wagons was nothing.

But if everyone could afford one — like Beatrice says — what then?

"Charlie, what about Papa's business?" The question comes out sounding like a croak, full of my worries.

Charlie stops caressing his miniature automobile and

39

puts it in his pocket. He takes me by the arm and quietly says, "Emily, this is only a toy. Your papa is still making lots of carriages."

I can't think of any words to make the uncomfortable air between us disappear.

Charlie tries again. "Bea Pea doesn't know everything. Even if some folks start buying automobiles, it'll take years and years before your pa has to worry about his business. Look how long it has been since Ben Franklin discovered electricity. Most folks still don't have it."

I brighten. "You're right, Charlie." The vise around my chest loosens with relief.

"It takes a long time for things to change. So don't let Bea Pea ruin your day."

If Miss Carlisle hadn't rung the bell ending recess, I would have given Bea Pea a piece of my mind. Obsolete, indeed. I wonder what obsolete means.

I ask Papa at supper.

"Obsolete means no longer in use. Out of date. Where did you hear the word, Emily?"

I don't want to hurt Papa's feelings by telling him what Beatrice said. Besides, it was Beatrice after all, and Charlie was right about electricity. "I heard it at school."

"Can you think of anything that's obsolete?" Papa asks.

I shake my head and say, "No. But I know something that will never be obsolete."

"What?" asks Papa.

"Your carriages."

Papa sighs and looks at Mama across the table. He holds up his glass of milk and says, "I'll drink to that."

When Mama joins us in the toast, her brow is wrinkled and her lips pressed together like she wants to say something but doesn't want to spoil the moment.

"Is something the matter, Mama?"

"Nothing beyond the usual worries." She smiles, but I can tell her heart isn't in it.

"Ella, do you have any plans for Emily tomorrow?"

I am grateful to Papa for changing the subject. I think Mama is too, because she gets up to fetch Papa's coffee.

She stares at Papa with questions in her eyes. "I can always find something for her to do." This time Mama smiles at me with a twinkle in her eye, so I know she's teasing. But I smile back just in case.

Papa is not saying anything, but he has a look about him like he knows a secret that he's dying to tell. At least, that's how Charlie looks when he has a secret.

Mama sighs and shakes her head. "What do you have planned, John?"

"I'll be going to the train station to pick up some parts for a new carriage. Thought Emily might give me a hand."

"Can I, Mama?" Papa has never asked me along when he goes to pick up supplies. Maybe he finally realizes I'm serious about the carriage business. "I'll be a big help and —"

"— And you can pick up some things for me at the market while you're there," Mama says.

"Sure, Mama."

"I want to go, Papa," William begs.

Papa lifts William onto his lap. "When you get to be Emily's size, you can be my helper. For now, you have to stay here and take care of Mama."

"How do I do that?" William pouts.

"By being a good lad and listening to what Mama says." Papa takes William's chin in his strong hand. "You can do that, can't you, son?"

William sniffles and nods. "Yes, Papa."

Papa sets William onto his feet and says, "Well then, for taking on such an important job, I'm putting you in charge of the key." Papa pulls an old skeleton key out of his trouser pocket.

William's eyes sparkle like morning dew on the grass. "This key opens every door in the house," he tells William. "Put it in a safe place."

William clutches the key in his small fist. "I won't never lose it." He runs to the kitchen door and tries it out.

Mama shakes her head and says, "I hope you realize he's going to be opening and closing doors all day."

It's a short ride from our house to the Baltimore and Ohio train station. This area along the tracks — and the neighborhood surrounding the White House — are the only places in DC with electricity. Even Charlie's house, four blocks away from ours, has gas lighting. Papa says electricity makes it easier to work after dark if he needs to. Mama says to have electricity is a luxury and a blessing.

My heart beats faster as we pull into the station. There is so much busy excitement about this place. Freight trains bringing all sorts of goods and, at another station stop, passenger trains taking people wherever they want to go. Folks arrive from faraway places I've only read about. New York,

Chicago, and San Francisco.

My senses perk up as we pass the open-air markets with colorful fruits and vegetables. The smells of smoked meats, cheese, fresh bread and cakes all make my mouth water. A less appetizing aroma comes from a stand of fresh fish from the Potomac River. Purveyors offer coffee, teas, lemonade, root beer, and Coca-Cola. Stronger spirits for adults, and ice cream sodas for anyone. If I spent a whole day smelling and tasting my way through the markets, I wouldn't make even a dent.

Papa and I share a glass of lemonade and a piece of chocolate fudge. We like the fudge so much, Papa buys some for Mama and William.

After Papa and I load up the wagon with the things he ordered for the new carriage, I ask him the question that has been bubbling inside me since last night.

"Papa, why did you bring me with you today?"

"So you could help." He lifts me onto the wagon seat and climbs in beside me.

"You never asked for my help before," I say.

"If you didn't want to come, all you had to do was say so."

"No, Papa, I'm glad you invited me. I was just wondering why this time."

Papa smiles a naughty smile, like Charlie does when we're doing something we're not supposed to. He swats Colonel with the reigns and we head to the General Store for the last few items on Mama's list.

"What's so special about this time, Papa?"

"I was going to keep it a secret until the carriage was done, but knowing you, you'd probably wheedle it out of Sam or Henry before long anyway." He looks at me, still smiling. "I haven't even told your mama yet."

"Who is the carriage for?"

"An important person in Washington."

"More important than Mr. Sousa?" My head spins thinking of who it could be.

"You might say he's the most important person in these parts."

I sigh in frustration. "Papa, I can't think of anybody except maybe President Roosevelt, so give me another clue."

Papa chuckles. "You don't need another clue."

When I realize what he means, I get so tingly with excitement, I want to jump from the wagon and dance down the road. "You're making a carriage for the president of the United States!"

Papa nods in his quiet way.

I feel so full of pride for Papa. Now I know for sure that Beatrice was wrong about carriages being obsolete. A carriage for the president of the United States is proof enough for me. "Your carriage will be more special and beautiful because President Roosevelt will ride in it."

Papa says nothing, but his head is high and the air around us seems to sing. I feel like the wagon might sprout wings and lift us skyward, like the fanciful contraption made by the Wright Brothers that Miss Carlisle told us about. Then again, looking at Papa, I realize you don't need wings to fly.

CHAPTER 7

Before the week is out, nearly everyone in town knows that Papa is building a carriage for the president. It's a good thing Papa told Mama about it when we returned from the train station. I figured once she knew, it was okay for me to tell Charlie.

I should have waited until we were alone to tell him. But the thrill of it blew away my good sense. I told him after school as we got ready to go home.

All Charlie could say was, "The president himself?"

"Yes! So that proves that carriages are not obsolete." I glare at Beatrice as she walks past us.

Charlie nods. "The president sure wouldn't waste his time ordering a carriage if he wasn't going to use it."

"Your father is making a carriage for Mr. Roosevelt?" Beatrice asks.

"Yes, he is," I say. "Our president appreciates the value of well-made things."

"So what?" Beatrice says. "He's not going to be our president much longer."

"What do you mean?"

"I happen to know for a fact they'll be electing a new president in a few weeks."

"What does that have to do with anything?"

"He's still president now," Charlie says.

"Yes he is, and he's a very important man, and what business is it of yours, anyway?" I want to throw something at Beatrice. Where's a good pie when you need one?

She smirks and says, "It's fitting that the old president goes out with the old carriage."

So, thanks to Beatrice's eavesdropping and that conversation, the new telephone Papa put in the kitchen hasn't stopped ringing with folks asking if Papa met Mr. Roosevelt. Do he and Mr. Roosevelt dine together? Are they boyhood friends? How can they get an invitation to the White House to meet the president?

Mama hangs up the telephone and says, "Emily Soper, you ought to be ashamed of yourself for all this nonsense and time wasting." She shakes her head. "I'm beginning to think your papa used poor judgment telling you about the carriage."

I sigh, my heart heavy with shame for causing such bother. "I'm sorry, Mama. I was just so proud of Papa and wanted Charlie to know. I didn't expect Beatrice Busybody to tell the world."

"Maybe it's a lesson learned. Proper young ladies

don't gossip or boast." She looks at me, hands on hips. "All this foolishness has me behind in my work. I want you to iron Papa's shirts and handkerchiefs. You've watched me enough to know what to do."

"Yes, Mama." I wrap the thick pressing cloth around the board and set it on the table. I take one of Papa's starched white shirts and spread it out over the board. I lift the hot iron from the stove and run it over the shirt, pressing out the wrinkles. After getting a spot smoothed over, I press another part. By the time I finish, the first part wrinkles again and I have to start over.

I switch to handkerchiefs. There are a couple of Mama's lacy ones, but most all the hankies belong to Papa. I unroll one of the still-damp squares. After doing one and setting it over the chair to stay wrinkle-free, I suddenly get a thought that makes me frown.

"Mama, what's the point of ironing all these hankies when Papa is just going to blow snot in them and stuff them in his pocket?"

"Emily Soper!" Mama's eyes flash, and her voice booms at me with such force, it reminds me of one of the firecrackers Charlie lit at last year's Independence Day celebration.

"What did I do, Mama?" I sigh and rest the iron on the hankie.

"More like what came out of that mouth of yours." She comes up real close, so she's looking me right in the eye.

"I will not have such unladylike language coming from any daughter of mine. I've a mind to wash your mouth out with some of this soap." She waves the bar in the air and I don't doubt for a minute that she'd do it.

"It . . . just slipped out. I'm sorry." I am sorry I said snot out loud. Though it seems like a harmless enough word compared to some of the zingers Charlie sometimes lets out.

Still, ironing hankies seems like one of those silly jobs that have no purpose. Like scrubbing the outhouse. It's only going to get dirty and smelly again.

"Let this be your warning." Mama puts down the soap and goes back to kneading the bread dough.

I breathe a little easier. Until I lift up the iron and see a perfect brown impression of it imprinted on the hankie. I sniff the air. Is Mama going to smell the scorch?

I quickly stuff the hankie in the pocket of my dress before she has a chance to notice it. I tell myself to calm down. Mama's so busy, she can't possibly notice my red face or hear my racing heart.

William runs in holding something in his chubby fist. I let out a breath of relief since he's just saved my hide. He's trying to squeeze past Mama, so I'll bet he's hiding some kind of critter.

"What do you have in your hand, William?" Mama asks.

"Nuffin'."

I swear Mama must have eyes in the back of her head. Did Mama notice the scorch? I sniff the air again, straining to smell anything out of the ordinary.

I can stand here and get worked up with worry that Mama did notice the scorch and is saving up her anger for later. Or I can make things easier for Will by finding out what he's hiding before Mama does.

Both of us will be better off if we slip outside for a moment.

"I'll be right back, Mama," I say.

"Where are you going? You still have work to do."

"I'm going to take Will to the privy." I grab William's empty hand and lead him outside.

"Open your hand," I say.

Will shakes his head and hides his fist behind his back.

"Will, I want to see it," I insist.

He opens his fist and there's the tiniest mouse I've ever seen. No bigger than a walnut.

Dead as a walnut too.

"Where did you get this, Will?"

"I found it under Mama's rose bush. A black cat bit it. I poked the cat with a stick and it ran away. He's sleeping so nice, Emmie. I'm going to make him a bed from Mama's matches box." He frowns. "Mama will let me keep him, won't she?"

"I don't think so."

"Why not?" He looks about ready to cry.

"You know Mama and critters. Besides, this is a baby and it needs its own mama." I don't have the stomach to tell him it's dead.

"But I saved him." William sniffs.

"And that was very brave. But how would you feel if someone took you away from your mama?"

"I'd really miss her."

"Sure you would. Same with this little fellow. So we're going to bring him back to his mama."

"How?"

"We'll put him where you found him so his mama can come get him. She probably left him there to look for food." I feel like a rat lying to Will, but I'd feel like a bigger rat if I made him cry by telling him the mouse was dead.

Will shows me the spot under the rose bush. I scoop up a small mound of dirt.

"Go ahead and lay him down," I say.

A big, fat tear rolls down Will's cheek as he kisses the mouse on its tiny head. Then he sets it down in the hole.

"How long before his mama comes?" he asks.

"I expect she'll be around soon enough. But she won't come while we're standing here. You have to promise not to bother this spot or poke around in it, or else the mama mouse may not come back."

Will nods his head. "What if he gets cold waiting?"

He can't get much colder is what I think. What I say is, "Why don't you cover him with this hankie and a little dirt to keep him warm?" I feel like biting off my own tongue for being so deceitful.

I help him wrap the mouse in the scorched hankie. It needs burying as much as the mouse does. Will scoops up a fist full of dirt and gently covers the mouse with it.

"Bye, Mousie. Your mama will be here soon." He pats the small mound and lets out a shaky sigh.

He looks so sad, it just about breaks my heart. "How would you like a piggyback ride around the house?" I say.

That is all it takes to bring the spark back into Will's eyes.

I run around the house twice just to make sure his good feeling lasts.

Back to the ironing, I try to be extra careful, hoping Mama forgot about my slip of the tongue. I feel uncomfortable with the quiet, especially after scorching the hankie and burying it with the mouse, so I ask Mama a question I've been thinking about for a while.

"Mama, do you think Mr. Roosevelt is a good president?"

"He seems to be a good family man. Papa is sorry he won't be running for reelection."

"If he was running, would you vote for him?"

"Don't talk foolishness, Emily. You know women aren't allowed to vote."

"It's not fair," I say.

"A lot of things in life aren't fair," Mama says.

"Don't you think women should have a say in how the government does things?" I ask. "Since men make the rules, everything seems to be in their favor."

"Which only makes it harder to change something like women's suffrage," Mama says. "Men like to know they're in charge of things. And some men don't think women are smart enough to make good decisions."

"That's plain wrong. You have to decide so many things every day. And why would a man think his own wife wasn't smart? I can't see how that makes for a happy household."

Mama sighs and her whole body seems to deflate when she says, "Some battles are too big and hard to fight."

"But if no one ever fights, nothing will change." My breath catches as I realize I've just discovered a change I would like to see.

"It's the way the world is." Mama lifts the iron out of my hand and puts it back on the stove to get hot. "Pay attention. You nearly scorched Papa's shirt." She hands me a smaller iron for pressing the cuffs.

Mama brushes a loose strand of hair off her forehead,

then goes back to kneading bread dough.

Mama works just as hard as Papa does, only things never stay done. When Papa makes a carriage, it will stay built and useful for a long while. All the things that Mama does — washing, scrubbing, polishing, sewing, ironing, cooking — no sooner get done than they have to be done again.

We don't have servants like Beatrice's family does. Papa calls the Peabody family "well-to-do." That's the same as being rich. But it seems to me that if all the ladies held a strike like the miners did last summer, things would change pretty quickly. I bet girls could even be blacksmiths if we wanted to.

"What would happen if all the ladies stopped cleaning, cooking, and taking care of their men?" I ask.

"I'm sure men wouldn't stand for it. They have their own work and so do women. Society needs order to function properly."

Mama rarely complains about all the things she has to do. She seems satisfied with things being the way they are. Still, a thought pokes at me, sharp and unexpected like a needle.

"Aren't some things worth fighting for, Mama? Like being able to choose your own path in life? Miss Carlisle says the freedom the Founding Fathers fought for only protects half the population. Until women vote, they'll never be truly free. She says it's a change that is coming and she welcomes it. Do you, Mama?"

Mama stops kneading and quietly says, "It won't matter for me, but I hope it happens for you."

I feel like my heart just grew twice its size. "Oh Mama, it makes me so happy to hear you say that."

"Until that day comes, there's still ironing to be done."

She goes back to punching dough with a bit more enthusiasm than before.

I finish pressing shirts, my dress, and our bedsheets. Mama is ready to give me another job of sweeping and scrubbing the privy — the absolute worst job — when someone knocks at the door.

"Answer that, Emily. Tell whoever it is we have no information about the president."

But it isn't anybody asking questions, just Sam asking me to come help in the barn.

Mama points to the stove. "Take the biscuits and a jar of jam. I suspect you all are hungry."

I pack everything in a basket and we head out to the barn. "What do you want me to do?" I ask.

Sam drags a crate out from under the table. "After you serve these good-smelling biscuits and bring fresh water for coffee, you can sort this crate of nuts, bolts, and screws. When you're finished, bring them back to me so I can figure out what I need for the upholstery."

It's easy work. It could be done in no time, but I make a game of it. I listen to the barn's jumble of sounds, sorting them out in my head.

A ping from Henry's hammer and I drop a screw in its box. The back-and-forth buzz of Sam's saw gets a nut and bolt. Buzz, buzz, ping. Nut, bolt, screw. Ping, buzz, buzz. Screw, nut, bolt. I'm so busy concentrating, I don't see Papa until he says, "Under that messy tomboy is a meticulous worker."

"What does meticulous mean?"

"To do a job carefully. To take pride in it."

"Papa, you, Henry, and Sam are the most meticulous

people I know."

Papa smiles and leaves me to finish my sorting. When I'm done, I take the boxes back to Sam.

"Thank your ma for the biscuits," Sam says. "They were mighty tasty."

"Do you need anything else?" I want to linger as long as I can.

"You can hand me those shears." He points to a large pair of clippers hanging on the wall.

I hand him the shears. "Are you excited about helping Papa make a carriage for Mr. Roosevelt?" I ask.

"Honey, I'm excited about every carriage I work on." Sam smiles. "I consider myself lucky to get paid for what I love doing."

"Emily, I hope you're not bothering Sam," Papa says. He looks at the boxes I sorted. "You did a fine job. Go on home now. I'll let you know if I need you again."

I stop by the forge on the way out. "Hi, Henry. Isn't it exciting?"

"Isn't what excitin'?"

"Making a carriage for the president!"

Henry takes a sip of coffee and sets his cup down with a shaky hand. Watching him has me worried. I've never seen his hands shake in all the time I've spent in the barn.

"Well, Miss Emily, I guess some folks would be excited workin' for the president. He's an important man, all right. But I get excited every time I start a job."

"That's what Sam said."

Henry wipes his forehead with the back of his hand. He sits on his stool, resting his head against a big post. "Is it cold outside, Miss Emily? I'm feelin' the chill of winter." He shivers as he reaches for the coffee cup.

My worry bubbles and churns inside me like boiling water. Winter or not, no one should feel chilly next to the heat of the forge.

"Are you okay, Henry?"

Henry shakes his head. "I don't think so. Hand me that bucket."

Before I can get it to him, Henry pukes up the coffee onto the floor.

"Papa, help!" I scream, afraid to leave Henry alone, but more afraid of doing nothing.

As Papa rounds the corner, Henry falls off his stool and collapses in a heap on the floor.

CHAPTER 8

I hold Henry's hand while Papa calls Dr. Harrison. Henry opens his eyes, mumbles some words, and closes his eyes again. His skin is so hot, it could bend iron on its own. We set his head on a pillow and cover him with a bolt of cloth, afraid to move him.

When Dr. Harrison arrives, Papa brings him to the forge where Henry lies.

Dr. Harrison takes one look at Henry and says, "You have misled me, Mr. Soper."

"How have I misled you?" Papa asks.

"You did not inform me that the patient was colored."

"What difference does that make?" Papa's face is so full of anger, it looks like he might hit the doctor.

Dr. Harrison adjusts the glasses on his nose and clears his throat. "I have many patients to look after. I don't make it a policy to treat those who are better served by doctors in their own neighborhoods."

Papa stares at Dr. Harrison over the top of his glasses. It's the same stare he uses when he is disappointed with my behavior. The longer Papa stares, the more Dr. Harrison clears his throat, yanks on his shirt collar, and adjusts his own glasses.

In his calmest voice Papa says, "I'm sure Mr. Jackson would prefer his own doctor if he were in his own neighborhood. Since he is here, and in desperate need of care, you will have to do. If you don't have the expertise or qualifications to properly examine him, then perhaps I should look for another doctor for our family."

"Now just a moment, Mr. Soper." Dr. Harrison's face turns redder as he stutters and stammers and tries to talk his way out of the mess he's fallen into by opening his mouth instead of his heart.

Papa's hands are in fists at his side.

I swear I can almost see steam rising off his skin, he's that angry. If I had Mama's fly swatter, I'd take a good whack at Dr. Harrison. How can he stand there making excuses when Henry is on the floor?

"What kind of a doctor are you? Do something." I know I shouldn't have said it out loud because now Dr. Harrison and Papa are staring at me. But it's as if they've forgotten that Henry is lying on the floor.

"My daughter is not normally rude. She speaks that way because she cares deeply for all of God's creatures. I thought you felt the same."

Dr. Harrison's jaw moves up and down like he's chewing something hard, but his mouth stays shut. He takes off his coat, opens his medical bag, and begins to examine Henry.

"It looks like pneumonia. A serious case." Dr. Harrison says. "He'll need bed rest, fluids, and steam to help clear out the lungs. Here's some codeine if he coughs." He hands Papa a bottle from his bag.

Papa walks Dr. Harrison outside. They say something to each other, look back in my direction, and then Dr. Harrison holds out a hand for Papa to shake. It's a long minute before Papa shakes it and the doctor leaves.

"Emily . . ." Papa says when he returns.

"I'm sorry I was disrespectful to Dr. Harrison, Papa, but he kept making excuses and Henry . . ."

Papa holds a hand up to stop me. "While I don't condone talking back to adults, I believe your comments were the catalyst Dr. Harrison needed to spring into action."

"Catalyst?"

"An action that brings about a result."

He and Sam lift Henry into a wagon, wrap blankets around him, and take him to our house. Mama makes a bed for him on the sofa in the parlor.

The Jacksons don't have a telephone, so Papa rides out to Henry's neighborhood to let Mrs. Jackson know.

When he returns, he tells Mama that Mrs. Jackson wants Henry brought home so she can look after him herself. Papa doesn't think it's a good idea to move Henry.

"Did you tell her we're glad to care for him here?" Mama asks.

Papa sighed. "She said he was her responsibility. She wants to care for him at home where he belongs." Papa frowns. "She also mentioned that it's inappropriate for him to stay in this neighborhood."

"Why, Papa? What's wrong with our neighborhood?"

Papa's face looks pained as he says, "While it makes no difference to me, some of our neighbors would object to a man of color sleeping under our roof."

"Who cares what the neighbors think?" I say. It makes no sense how some folks hang on to hateful ideas and beliefs as if they were medals of honor, to be polished and displayed with pride.

We wrap Mama's heavy quilt around Henry, and Papa and Sam put him in the wagon.

"That should keep the worst wind off him," Mama says. "Here's another blanket to cover him." Mama's face wrinkles in worry. "How's she going to manage with four little ones, two not yet in school?" She shakes her head. "Emily, help me load some food for supper. Last thing Mrs. Jackson needs to worry about is what to cook."

I help Mama fill a basket with biscuits, cheese, and the pot of beef stew we were going to eat.

"Those little ones need a hot meal more than we do," Mama says.

When Papa returns, he and Sam head right to the barn. "Why didn't Papa come back and tell us how Henry is?" I ask Mama. I can see the barn all lit up from the kitchen window.

"I expect Papa has a lot of work to catch up on since most of the day was spent tending to Henry." Mama takes a new batch of biscuits from the oven. "Set the table for you and William."

I don't have much of an appetite. My head is dizzy with worry for Henry and Papa. With Henry so sick, who will help Papa make the carriage for Mr. Roosevelt?

"Is Henry going to be okay, Mama?" I set the plates on the kitchen table.

"Pneumonia is a serious thing." Mama looks at me. She sighs and puts a hand on my shoulder. "I know you're worried, Emily. Maybe if you say a little prayer for Henry you'll feel better. Folks can always use a prayer." She kisses my forehead and says, "Help your brother wash for supper."

I say two prayers. One for Henry and another for Papa.

Chapter 9

Papa never works on Sunday. Except for the farmers who tend their livestock, folks consider Sunday the Lord's day and time to rest from work.

Depending on the weather, Papa sometimes takes us on a carriage ride around town. We've visited the Smithsonian Museum and the Washington Monument. We even walked up all 898 steps to the top, Papa carrying William on his shoulders. Papa had to sit and rest a couple of times on the way up, but once we got to the top, it was a thrill to look out at the trees and roads below. It was like being a bird and seeing everything for miles around.

This Sunday we are going to visit Henry and his family.

Henry lives in a neighborhood of DC called Shaw. We drive past shops and businesses. There are a lot of small farms and gardens and houses where one is attached to another. I've never seen this part of Washington.

"Papa, how come we haven't been here before?" I'm sitting next to Papa. Mama and William are in the back of the carriage with the things we are bringing to Henry's family.

"There hasn't been a need for us to come here before this," he says.

There aren't many carriages in this neighborhood. Many folks ride bicycles; people are on foot pulling carts and wagons. Delicious Sunday supper smells are coming out of some open windows, and a few dogs bark as we pass. The houses are closer together here than in our neighborhood, but the yards are neat and tidy and the stoops are swept clean. When we get in front of Henry's house I notice something else.

"Papa, why is everyone staring at us?"

Papa lets out a heavy sigh, like there's a weight pressing on him and it's hard to breathe.

"I imagine white folks don't come to this part of DC on a Sunday."

My stomach flips and my heart speeds up. "Is it wrong for us to be here?"

"No," Papa explains. "Some folks might feel uneasy wondering why we're here with no business to conduct."

"We're here to help Henry's family," I say.

"That's right. There is no wrong time to help a friend."

Until right this minute, I never thought about why there are no colored folks in our part of town. Would Henry live closer to us if he could?

This seems like a nice, quiet neighborhood. I wouldn't mind living here. As long as folks are kind to each other, what difference does it make where you live? I think of Dr. Harrison and how he didn't want to examine Henry because his skin is brown. I know Dr. Harrison wouldn't want to live here or have Henry living next door to him. Some educated people sure are ignorant.

Papa brings the carriage to a stop. He steps down and helps me off the seat. We tie up Colonel to a hitching post and unload the carriage.

When Mrs. Jackson opens the door, her eyes widen in surprise.

"I wasn't expecting company," she says, touching her hair and smoothing out her apron. "I must look a fright."

"We don't mean to bother you, Mrs. Jackson," Mama says. "We thought you might need a few things."

"Pardon my manners, Mr. and Mrs. Soper. Please come in." She looks at me. "You must be Emily. Henry's always talking about you." She smiles a nervous kind of smile as we walk through the door. "Your son's name is?"

"William," Mama says.

"Hello," says William.

The smile Mrs. Jackson gives William relaxes her face. She calls out, "Samuel, Joseph, Alice, we have company." At the sound of their names, three children appear.

Samuel is eight, Joseph six, Alice four, and the baby Abraham is one and napping in his cradle in a warm corner of the kitchen. The boys wear overalls and cotton shirts. Alice wears a plaid cotton dress. The clothes are faded and worn, but clean and pressed.

The boys favor Mrs. Jackson; each has a dimple on his right cheek like her. Alice looks like Henry with a quiet smile and black eyes. I like them already, just by the sight of them.

Samuel keeps glancing at the closed door where I suspect Henry is. He's biting on his lip, and Joseph is chewing his fingernail, so I know they're worried. Alice stands quiet and still, examining me and William. I guess she's wondering if we're friendly. I smile and give her a small wave. She steps behind her mama, peeking.

"Children, take William into the parlor and show him how to play checkers." Mrs. Jackson looks at me. "You may join them if you like, Emily."

"May I stay here?"

She nods and offers us seats.

"How is Henry?" Papa asks as we sit down.

"No change. Sleeps fitful. Still feverish." She places a pot of water on the coal-fired stove. "I was about to boil water to steam up the room. Won't you have some tea and gingerbread?"

"Thank you," says Mama. "That's very kind. But please don't go to any trouble."

"No trouble, Mrs. Soper." She looks at Mama. "You made a delicious stew for us yesterday. Thank you."

"You're welcome." Mama smiles at her. "We brought a few more things."

Mrs. Jackson shakes her head. "You don't need to be worrying about us. I got a bit put aside until Henry's on his feet. Besides, we got good neighbors here. We look out for each other."

Mama and Mrs. Jackson eye each other for a long minute. Even though they aren't saying anything, there's a lot of communicating going on. The air around them seems suspicious, heavy and full of worry.

Charlie and I will sometimes stare at each other, trying not to laugh, seeing who can hold out the longest. With Mama and Mrs. Jackson though, I don't think anybody is going to laugh. I think they're trying to figure each other out.

When the water boils, Mrs. Jackson pours it into a basin and hands it to Papa. He nods and takes it into Henry's room.

Then Mrs. Jackson pours four cups of tea and cuts eight squares of gingerbread from a pan she removes from the icebox. She calls the children in and we all squeeze around the table.

This kitchen is smaller than ours, but it's clean and tidy and as warm as a piece of bread fresh from the oven. I like how the chairs are all different designs. Ours at home all match, which seems dull next to the variety here. Like everyone has a chair of his own. Special. I can't stop a smile when I see a horseshoe hanging over the door, just like the one I got from Henry.

Papa comes out of Henry's room and joins us. "He's awake and asking for a drink."

Mrs. Jackson pours another cup of tea and squeezes half a lemon into it. Then she spoons in a chunk of honeycomb and stirs.

"May I take it in?" Papa asks.

Mrs. Jackson favors Papa with a smile. "Henry enjoys working for you. Says you're a good man and fair. He respects you, Mr. Soper."

Papa returns her smile and says, "The feeling is mutual, Mrs. Jackson." Papa takes the tea to Henry.

We sit silently, eating gingerbread and staring at each

other. Mrs. Jackson stands at the counter, watching us without really looking at us. It's as if she's uncomfortable in her own kitchen. Which makes me feel like maybe we shouldn't be here. Maybe we should have waited until we were invited.

"This is delicious cake," Mama says, breaking the silence. "I've never had luck with gingerbread. Mine is always so crumbly. What's your secret?"

"A splash of vinegar in the batter makes all the difference," Mrs. Jackson says with pride.

"I never thought of that," says Mama.

And with that, the heaviness of the air is suddenly made lighter as Mama and Mrs. Jackson discuss recipes and cooking as if they've done so all their lives. The children giggle and tease each other, making silly faces. William loves this game and joins in. I don't know how it happened, but the kitchen now shimmers with a warm glow.

Most amazing of all, Mrs. Jackson and Mama are smiling.

When we're ready to leave, Mrs. Jackson accepts Mama's basket of oats, cheese, a meat loaf, apples, pickles, and a dozen turnips from the garden. They give each other a hug. "Bye, Ella." "Bye, Grace." they say.

Sitting next to Papa on the ride home, I ask, "What made Mrs. Jackson change her mind and accept Mama's basket?"

Papa shakes his head. "It's a conundrum, but I think both ladies swallowed a bit of pride along with that cake."

"Conundrum?"

"A puzzle or mystery," Papa says. He slaps Colonel with the reins and we're off.

"Figuring out how to be a proper grown-up is a conundrum," I say.

Papa smiles at me over his glasses. "You have no idea."

Things just aren't the same without Henry. The last two carriages are nearly finished and work is about to begin on the one for President Roosevelt. How can Papa make a carriage without a blacksmith?

The forge is quiet. A fire smolders in the hearth, but no one is there to make it blaze.

Papa promised Mr. Roosevelt he'd have his carriage before Christmas. Unless Henry gets better real soon, that won't happen.

Papa has to do something he doesn't want to do.

He must hire another blacksmith.

CHAPTER 10

"Won't Henry mind if someone else works in his forge?" I ask Papa. I've been in the barn every day after school, figuring Papa might need help with Henry gone.

"It was Henry's suggestion." Papa says nothing else, but by the way his broom drags over the floor, I can tell he is not happy replacing Henry.

"Tell Mama not to hold supper. I have to show the new man around and make sure he can handle the job." Papa's sigh is heavy, like he's already certain no one can measure up.

"You sure there's nothing I can do, Papa?"

Papa dismisses me with a wave of his hand and says, "I'll let you know if I need anything."

I meet Charlie on my way back to the house.

"What are you doing here on a Saturday?" I ask. "Don't you have chores?"

"I finished them. I came here to escape my pesky sisters. If they're not asking for piggyback rides or to play tag, they want me to sit for a tea party."

As much as I'd like to have a sister, four of them would make me want to run away too.

When we enter the kitchen, Mama has jobs for us.

"Beat the dust from the rugs I hung over the porch rail," Mama tells us. "Then take a bale of fresh straw and spread it out for Colonel. He needs oats and water. Sweep the stall before you lay the new straw. Put the old straw and manure in the compost pile."

"I know what to do, Mama. I always take care of Colonel."

"When you come back, hang up these wet sheets and towels while there's still some sunshine." Mama frowns. "Maybe you should do that first."

I roll my eyes at Charlie, who shrugs his shoulders. I've never seen Mama think in this many directions at once. "Don't worry, Mama. We'll get it done."

"Put on your boots and wear one of Papa's aprons so you don't get your dress dirty. I don't want to do any more laundry today. Even with this new electric washer and wringer, it takes all day. And no carriage barn."

I don't see the need to tell her I've already been there.

I hand Charlie the basket of wet sheets and towels, pick up the bag of clothespins, and hurry out the door while Mama stops to take a breath.

"What's your ma so worked up about?" Charlie asks as we pin the sheets to the clothesline stretched between two oak trees behind the house.

"I don't know." I look at Charlie. "With Henry sick

and Papa hiring a new blacksmith, I guess she's worried about getting the carriage done."

Charlie nods. "It's too bad about Henry. When will he be back?"

"We don't know." We hang up the last sheet and towels and head to the stable to take care of Colonel.

I brush Colonel's soft, coffee bean-brown coat with a currycomb while Charlie scoops the manure and old straw into a wheelbarrow. Colonel whinnies and nuzzles my arm to show his appreciation. Papa calls him a good old workhorse. To me, he's like a member of the family. He's been around as long as I can remember and I've been taking care of him since I was eight.

We spread out the fresh, sweet-smelling straw around the stall. I scoop out some oats from a barrel and fill up Colonel's feed bag. Charlie fills up a water bucket at the pump and dumps it into Colonel's trough. We put Colonel back in the stall and head for the garden to empty the wheelbarrow.

On the way, I remember the mouse Will found and tell Charlie about it.

Charlie's eyes are wide when I finish. "I remember all the dead critters me and my sisters found and buried in our garden patch. Pa says that's why the vegetables there are always so big. All that natural fertilizer. Finding the first one is pretty special, though."

"He was so proud, I didn't have the heart to tell him it wasn't sleeping."

"Let's see." Charlie gets on his hands and knees and digs in the spot I show him. "Are you sure this is where you buried it?"

"Positive," I say. "I wrapped it in the scorched hankie, figuring I could bury two mistakes at the same time."

Charlie stands up. "It's not there."

"Let me see."

I dig around the bush until I've exposed the roots and have Mama's roses close to falling down. I frown. "I know this is where we left it."

"Well, then some animal must have dug it up or . . ."

My heart skips a beat when I think of the "or."

"Will came back out and got it." I grab Charlie's arm. "If he took it inside after I told him not to, and Mama finds it . . ."

"Let's go talk to Will." Charlie suggests.

I hear honking and look up, sure that I'll see the Canada geese that spend winter here. The sky is clear and blue with not a bird in sight.

"Where's that honking coming from?" I say as I hear it again. This time there's shouting too.

"Sounds like it's coming from the street." Charlie sets the wheelbarrow down and says, "Let's go see."

When we get to the street in front of the house it looks like a parade. Neighbors are coming out of houses and lining up along both sides of the dirt road, shouting "Hello!" and "Did you hear that?" and "What's coming up the road?"

Mama and William come out of the house. "What on earth is that noise?" Mama asks.

"It's coming from that thing." Charlie points in the direction of the carriage coming toward us.

As it gets closer, I realize it's not a carriage at all.

"Is that what I think it is?" Charlie asks, jumping up and down. "It is, Will!" He hoists Will onto his shoulders and says, "It's one of Henry Ford's Model Ts." Charlie is all but dancing, he's that excited.

People holler and wave as the motorcar gets closer. It's shiny and black, but not as fancy as Papa's carriages. And it smells like a bunch of oil lamps all piled together and burning. How could anybody ride around with that foul smell following them?

As it passes in front of us, the horn honking gets louder, and I see none other than Beatrice in the front seat next to the driver.

"Hello, Charles and Emily!" she shouts. "This is my Uncle George's new automobile." Her face is pink from the chilly air and her eyes sparkle like they always do when she's full of herself. She waves to the bystanders as if she were a queen parading before her royal subjects. So like her mama.

Some folks cheer, others boo. Still others shake their heads and laugh. Folks ride bicycles or pull wagons behind the vehicle so it almost looks like a parade. A parade led by Beatrice Busybody riding Charlie's toy come to life.

And there's Charlie, rosy-cheeked and smiling, bouncing William on his shoulders and cheering as the Model T drives past. There's Mama, the worry wrinkles deep on her forehead. She looks at me and lets out a heavy sigh. I have an unsettled feeling in my stomach. Like I ate something disagreeable.

"Well, what do you think of that?" Charlie asks as he sets William on the grass.

"All that yelling and foolish nonsense," Mama says. "I'm surprised at Beatrice. I hope I never see you behave in such a vulgar fashion."

"Mama, I would never." I stop right there because I'm not sure which part of Beatrice's behavior offended her. And because I'm surprised Mama found fault with Beatrice to begin with. That girl has always been held up as a model of proper behavior.

"Have you finished your chores?" Mama asks.

I am so stunned and breathless by what I just witnessed, I can only nod.

"Well then, let's get back indoors, William, before you catch a cold in this chill."

"Wasn't that something?" Charlie says. "I'd give anything to ride in one of those."

"Would you?" Mean words burn my tongue, so I spit them out to get rid of the stinging. "Why don't you run after Bea Pea and ask for a ride? She's sweet on you, anyway. You two can be king and queen of the horseless carriage." I stomp off to the garden. I want to get away from Charlie's excitement, my own meanness, and the confusion whirling inside me.

"Emily!" I hear Charlie running behind me, but I don't turn around.

Charlie runs in front of me so I have to stop.

"Emily," he says over and over until I have to look him in the eye just to get him quiet. He says, "I don't care a fig about Bea Pea. Are you angry because I said it would be fun to ride in a Model T?"

"Don't you get it?" I am so hot it feels like July. Charlie just stares at me, waiting. I make him wait, trying to calm down.

"Get what?" he finally demands.

"If folks start riding automobiles, then what's going to happen to carriages? What will happen to Papa's business?" I let my worries spill out, fast and furious.

Charlie's mouth drops open. "I . . . I didn't think about . . . I didn't mean . . . Golly, I'm sorry, Emily." He looks so sad, I almost wish I hadn't yelled at him.

Suddenly his face brightens as he says, "It's just one automobile. Look how many carriages there are around here. Just because a person wants to ride an automobile doesn't mean he wants to own one. I want to ride a ship, a train, and a hot-air balloon. That doesn't mean I'm buying any of those things. It's like those rides at the carnival." His eyes beg me to forgive and understand.

It's hard to stay mad at Charlie. I know sometimes I let my worries take over common sense. If Mama thought the whole thing was nonsense, then it must be. I shouldn't let Beatrice and her stupid ideas upset me.

"I guess you're right. It is just one automobile and there are thousands of carriages." I sigh, blowing out all the bad feelings into the air. "I'm sorry I yelled at you, Charlie."

"That's okay," he says, smiling. "I get carried away thinking about all the changes going on. Pa says it's a fine time to be growing up and a witness to it all."

"You and your papa are excited about the changes?" I remember the talk Papa and I had a few weeks back about not wanting things to change at all. Papa was right about some things happening whether we want them to or not. Why can't people be content with the way things are?

Stupid change.

"I can't wait to see what the world will be like when I'm a man." Charlie's blue eyes are dreamy and faraway as he thinks about his future. "Don't you ever wonder about things like that?" he asks.

It's hard for me to admit, but there's a small part of me that is just as excited as Charlie. The part of me that wonders what it would be like to ride in a Model T. Charlie doesn't wait for me to answer.

"Enough of the future. I'm getting hungry," he says. "Let's finish the chores so we can get an ice cream soda at the drugstore."

"You got money?"

He nods and grins. "I found five cents in the dirt on the way over here." He takes a coin out of his pocket, tossing it in the air. "Heads or tails?" he asks, catching the coin.

"Heads," I say as Charlie slaps the nickel onto the back of his hand.

"You win."

"What do I win?" I'm excited even though I don't know the prize.

"You get to pick the ice cream flavor."

As we race to the backyard, I don't feel angry anymore. The confused feeling is worse, though. Now I can't get rid of the image of Charlie and me riding in one of those stupid Model Ts.

CHAPTER 11

When Charlie and I get to the drugstore, there's a crowd of people standing around the streets. We have to push our way to the door. It's not just men like it usually is on a busy Saturday. There are ladies all dressed up and children running around. Some folks are waving flags like they do on Independence Day. The air feels charged and crackly as if we were in a lightning storm.

"What's going on?" I ask Mr. Anderson, the druggist.

"They're having a political rally for Mr. Taft," Mr. Anderson says.

"Right here?" Charlie asks.

"No. But last we heard, they're coming through town on the way to the train station. The president, some senators, and members of Congress are trying to drum up votes for their favorite candidate."

"The president is riding through here?" I look at Charlie. "Wouldn't it be grand to see Mr. Roosevelt?"

"It sure would," Charlie agrees. "I've never met anyone famous before."

Charlie and I move outside. Spectators line the sidewalk on both sides of the street. I can't find a good place for us to stand.

"If the president passes by, I won't be able to see him." I sigh.

"Just a minute." Charlie runs behind the store. He returns with a wooden crate that he turns upside down for us to stand on. I still can't see over the heads of men and women with their fancy hats, but I can peek under hats and over shoulders to see down the street.

A marching band starts playing and flags wave as the crowd gets louder with shouts and cheers.

"Here they come!" someone yells.

"Where?" I say. "Can you see anything, Charlie?"

"Not yet."

I watch and listen. Soon heads shift to the right a bit, so I know something is coming from that direction. I peek under the hat of a bearded man smoking a cigar. I guess I lean in a bit too close because he says, "Young lady, kindly stop breathing down my neck." He blows out a puff of cigar smoke that leaves a little cloud in the air.

"Sorry, mister." I cough and flap my arms to clear the air of the awful smell.

Charlie elbows me and we laugh.

Then I see the carriages all decked out with flags, bunting in red, white, and blue, and banners that say ELECT

TAFT FOR PRESIDENT. One horse even has a sign attached to its blanket. People cheer and wave.

"What's going on? Do you see Mr. Roosevelt?" I ask Charlie. My heart beats faster at the thought of seeing him.

"I see lots of men," Charlie says. "None of them look like the president. Something is happening across the street."

"What?"

"I don't know for sure. It looks like some ladies holding up signs."

The mood of the crowd has shifted as cheering is replaced by hissing and booing.

Charlie spots an opening in the crowd and we jump off the crate so we can wiggle our way through to the front. A group of women are holding signs calling for women's suffrage. They're women of all ages, and right in the middle of the dozen or so brave souls is Miss Carlisle.

"Charlie, do you see. . .?"

"I know. It's Miss Carlisle. Can you believe it?" Charlie seems just as excited as I am. After the talk I had with Mama about women getting the right to vote, it's encouraging to see real women trying to change something that's unfair.

"I wonder why Miss Carlisle never mentioned this rally," I say.

My question gets answered in a very unpleasant way when, out of nowhere, some young men riding by in a wagon viciously toss buckets of pig slop at the suffragists.

I hear things like "It's an abomination" and "Unnatural behavior." It sure is. Young men shouldn't behave like that.

Sadly, I realize the men on the edges of the crowd are

talking about the suffragists. One says, "If my woman acted like that, I'd take her over my knee and give her a whipping until she came to her senses."

Another man says, "Women need to remember their place is in the home taking care of the family, not disgracing themselves in public."

The worst of all comes from none other than Mr. Peabody, Beatrice's father, who pronounces, "Women aren't smart enough to make political decisions."

By now the parade is gone, but the nasty hum of spectators still fills the air. The crowd begins to move. I don't even care if the president comes by now. I'm so worried that Miss Carlisle might be hurt.

Charlie grabs my hand and we make our way toward our teacher. Rotten vegetables litter the street. Many people ignore the suffragists as they pass by. Others make crude barnyard noises and hurl insults. Some ladies in the crowd look pained, yet they remain by their men as they walk away from the demonstrators.

Through it all, Miss Carlisle and the other suffragists stand tall, proud, and unflinching.

If only Mama could see this.

By the time we make it to the spot where the suffragists stood, they've all left. Charlie and I walk by a sign trampled in the dirt that reads: MEN VOTE TO DETERMINE THEIR FUTURE. WHY NOT WOMEN?

Charlie must read my mood because he says, "I hope Miss Carlisle is all right."

"Those women were so brave," I say.

"And foolish," adds Charlie.

"How can you say that? Don't you think your ma and other women should be allowed to vote?"

"I guess if they really want to, they should. But it's dangerous standing on the street like that. When the women got hit with all that rotten food, no one even tried to help them. And no one tried to stop it. They could have been hurt. That's plain foolish."

"You shouldn't blame the women for the men's bad behavior! Some of them acted like brutes, saying awful things."

Charlie frowns. "I wish I had a bucket of that slop! I'd toss it at those bums who did that to Miss Carlisle and her friends." He shakes a fist in the air.

I am reminded again why Charlie is my best friend.

Charlie sighs and says, "Let's go have our ice cream soda."

I decide not to mention anything to Mama about what happened to the suffragists. It might upset her if I do, and I've been doing too much of that lately.

CHAPTER 12

When I sneak into the barn after school on Monday, the new blacksmith startles me by barking, "Who are you?"

"I'm Emily Soper, sir."

"The boss's daughter. I heard about you."

He holds a hammer and a fresh, unbent piece of iron. I wait for him to introduce himself. He keeps his mouth shut and his eyes on me.

I know it isn't polite for a girl to be so bold with a grown-up, but I ask anyway. "What's your name?"

"Frederick Martin." He sticks the iron rod into Henry's fire pit. "Mr. Martin to you."

As if I don't know how to greet a grown-up.

"Nice to meet you, Mr. Martin," I say, even though I'm not sure it's nice at all.

He is taller than Henry. Older too, I figure, since he

has some streaks of gray in his brown hair. He's chewing loudly on something, working his jaws like he's chomping on gristle. While Henry smells like sweet hay and iron, Mr. Martin has a different smell. I'm not quite sure what it is, but it makes my stomach feel kind of funny.

Mr. Martin spits a black glob onto the floor of the forge. I've seen chewing tobacco before, just not in Henry's forge. Somehow it doesn't seem right.

"Would you like a bucket for your spit?" I say.

He doesn't answer. He stokes the fire with Henry's bellows. I watch the coals go from yellow to orange, then red.

"How long have you been a blacksmith? Are you working on the president's carriage? Is there anything I can do to help?"

He takes the rod from the coals and sets it on Henry's anvil. I wait to hear the hammer's song. Instead I hear this: "There is one thing that would help me. Stop asking questions and let me finish my work." He looks right at me and spits another glob that lands next to my shoe. It looks like a dead slug.

It's going to take more than that to make me leave.

I stand as quiet as a post, watching Mr. Martin work the iron. He doesn't stand up straight and proud like Henry. Mr. Martin leans over the anvil like he is trying to cover up something. Sort of like how Beatrice covers her papers at school, so no one can copy off her.

Like anyone would even want to.

I close my eyes and listen. Try as I might, the song of the forge is not the familiar one I usually hear. I sniff the air. As long as I don't stand near Mr. Martin, it smells the same.

The heat warms my face like it always does. Yet, when Mr. Martin hits the iron with Henry's hammer, it feels as if something is missing.

I realize the tapping has stopped and I open my eyes. Mr. Martin says, "Doesn't your mother have things for you to do? I'm busy and it's hard to concentrate with you standing there."

"Henry lets me watch."

"I'm not Henry. And, it isn't proper for a girl to be hanging around here."

Mr. Martin looks at me with his face all frowning and dark, like he sees something he's not pleased to look at. Or he ate something disagreeable. Or he's been sitting downwind of a pile of fresh manure. Then he goes back to chewing.

Papa appears with his brow worry-crinkled. "Please don't bother Mr. Martin, Emily."

"I was only watching, Papa."

"Some folks don't like being watched while they work. Run along."

I sigh. "Isn't there something I can do to help you, Papa?"

Papa looks at me over the top of his glasses.

"Okay. I'll go."

All the times I've been sent home from the barn never felt like this. It's as if the air that I breathe in there has been filled with something heavy and the good smells are turning bad. I miss Henry so much, it makes me dizzy.

CHAPTER 13

When I get back to the house, Mama hands me a quarter.

"Go to the drugstore for bicarbonate of soda. Then take these fruit jars to Mrs. Cook to swap for our weekly eggs, butter, and cream. Don't dawdle. I'm going to need the cream to make the cornbread for supper."

I skip along the dirt road with the basket on my arm, dodging piles of horse droppings that Charlie calls horse apples. A few grasshoppers leap from bayberry bushes as I brush by. A scrawny cat meows at me as it crosses the road. I am pleased to see wagons or carts in every yard I pass. Not one automobile to be found.

Maybe Beatrice and her rich uncle can afford to ride in one of Henry Ford's contraptions, but regular folks still want reliable horse-pulled vehicles. Then a worrisome thought pokes its way into my head.

Sure folks around here can't afford an automobile. These same folks can't afford Papa's carriages either. The people that buy from Papa are rich folks like Beatrice's family. And President Roosevelt. Maybe it's only a matter of time before those people decide to buy an automobile instead. Then what will happen to Papa's business?

By the time I get to the drugstore, my head is spinning and my stomach queasy from fretting.

As if my stomach isn't already turned upside down, I see Beatrice on a bench in front of the store. Standing next to her is her family's maid, Shirley.

Beatrice is frowning as if she'd rather be anywhere but on that bench. Shirley's pacing back and forth and holding a hankie to her face like she's about to cry.

I usually don't give a fig what Bea Pea says or does, but seeing Shirley in such a state makes me curious. Before they spot me, I scurry behind a rain barrel beside the store. I can't see them, but I can hear everything they say.

"Just one spool of white thread, Miss Beatrice. I got the dime right here." Shirley speaks in a chirpy voice that makes you think of a songbird. I'll bet she can sing like a songbird too.

"Buy it yourself," Bea Pea says. She sighs like she's got Henry's anvil resting on her shoulders.

"Miss Beatrice, you know I cain't go in there with your mama. She told me I don't belong in there."

"Then why didn't you ask Mama?"

"I didn't want to bother her!" Shirley protests. "But I bet she wouldn't think anything of it if you just went in there and —"

"Mama told me to stay right here and keep an eye on . . . things. Besides, don't you have stores in your own neighborhood?"

"They ain't got but cheap thread that's always breakin'. Costs twice as much too."

"And what do you think Mama would do to me if she found out I'm buying things for you?"

"You're her daughter. She let you do whatever you want."

"Hah. Is that what you think?"

"Miss Beatrice, why does your mama always make me come on these errands when I can't do no buying for myself, anyway? I got lots to do at the house. If I don't get the work done afore the day is out, she'll make a fuss and threaten to hold back my earnin's."

"Mama worries about you being alone in the house."

"I ain't afraid of being alone. She don't have to worry."

Beatrice makes a snorting sound and says, "That's not why she brings you along, you ninny."

I have never heard Beatrice use such an unkind word. I bet if Mrs. Peabody heard that, she'd wash Beatrice's mouth with soap. I know my mama would.

"Then why she drag me along every time? What? Is she afraid I'm going to steal somethin'?" Shirley laughs in a funny way, like she doesn't mean it.

Then it gets real quiet.

I peek my head around the barrel and can just see them. Bea Pea is twirling a lock of her hair so hard, it's a wonder it doesn't come loose from her head. I've never seen her with a curl out of place. Until now.

That's when I know Shirley answered her own question.

Mrs. Peabody thinks her own maid is a thief.

Shirley fidgets with the hankie and does a lot of coughing and throat clearing, like she's trying to choke down her own words.

Beatrice stops yanking on her curls and says, "I'd like to help, but I . . . It's just some silly thread. Hardly life or death. Now stop bothering me or I'll tell Mama."

Shirley's eyes get so big, you'd think she was looking at a ghost. "Please don't do that, Miss Beatrice."

"Then hush up." Beatrice goes back to worrying her poor hair.

Now what? I could just go into the drugstore and buy Mama's bicarbonate of soda as if I never heard anything.

Or I could tell Shirley I'll buy her the thread. But then Beatrice would tell the whole world that I'm a sneaky, eavesdropping busybody.

I suddenly get another idea. I walk around the back of the building, pretending I'm coming from the other direction. I march up the steps of the drugstore. Beatrice sees me, but she pretends not to, staring at her feet like they're the most fascinating things she's ever laid eyes on.

That's fine with me.

I enter the drugstore and see Mrs. Peabody first thing. It's hard to miss someone who's the loudest, largest, and most colorful object around. Flapping a yellow silk fan in front of her face, she's barking at Mr. Anderson, the druggist, as if he were deaf and dumb.

I move down an aisle to find what I'm looking for. Still, I can hear Mrs. Peabody's squawking.

"It's so stuffy in here, Harold. You really ought to

modernize this place with electric fans. They do wonders to the air. And when was the last time this place saw a coat of paint?" She shakes her head, flaps the fan faster, and adds, "How much longer is this going to take? I have other errands to run."

"Your order will be ready in a few minutes, Mrs. Peabody."

Mrs. Peabody stops flapping when I walk up to the counter. "Well, hello there, Emily. What a nice surprise. Is your mama here?" The word 'nice' comes out sounding like the hiss of a snake.

"No."

She's eyeing me up and down like I don't measure up to whatever standards she has in mind. Good thing her eyes aren't made of fire or they'd burn a hole right through me. I tuck Mama's basket of jams and peaches under my arm and smile politely.

"I'm surprised you're not running around outside on such a warm day, fooling with that Cook boy." She goes back to fan flapping.

Running around? Fooling? I can think of lots of rude things to say to that, but I remind myself why I'm here.

"Just getting something for Mama." I hand the spool of thread and my quarter to the girl at the cash register and accept the fifteen cents change.

"Give my regards to your mama," Mrs. Peabody says. "And tell Beatrice I'll be right out. Don't you two go running off anywhere."

I'd rather wrestle with a bobcat. "Yes, ma'am," I say through clenched teeth and walk out the door.

Beatrice and Shirley are still outside. I walk up to Beatrice. "Your mama says she's nearly done."

She gives me the same stare her mama did.

"Hi, Shirley." I smile. A real one this time.

"Hello, Miss Emily." Shirley smiles back.

Now that I have their attention, I make a big deal out of looking in the basket and say, "Oh, darn. I think I just bought Mama the wrong thread." I hold it in my palm in front of Shirley. "This isn't ivory, is it?" I frown.

"It's white," says Shirley.

"The light was bad in the store. I guess I'm going to have to go back in and exchange it." I sigh, loud and heavy like the whole idea of it is more than I can bear.

"Wait, Miss Emily. I have a need for white thread. May I buy it off you?" Shirley holds her dime out.

"Really?" I say. "That would be grand. Then I don't have to feel silly going back in there." I hand her the thread. She gives me the dime, tucking the spool of thread into her burlap satchel.

With no time to spare, Mrs. Peabody comes out the door.

We must look guilty because she gives all three of us the eye and says, "What have you been up to, Beatrice?"

"Nothing, Mama." Beatrice turns a bright shade of pink and starts torturing her hair until she remembers her mama is watching her. Then she tucks her hands into the folds of her dress. Her eyes are here, there, and everywhere except on her mama.

"Well then, let's run along, shall we? Your daddy will be picking us up soon, and we still have to go to the butcher."

Mrs. Peabody dismisses me with a nod, grabs Beatrice

by the arm, and all but drags her down the road. Shirley gives me a small wave before following behind them like an obedient puppy.

I am so stunned, I can hardly move.

First, to discover how Mrs. Peabody treats poor Shirley.

The bigger shock is seeing a side of Beatrice I've never seen before. Where is the bragging, know-it-all, full-of-herself girl I see every day at school? Around her mama, Beatrice acts like a piece of bacon in a hot skillet. Twitchy, shriveled, and simmering. Just about ready to pop.

If I didn't know better, I'd swear Beatrice is afraid of her own mama.

Can you imagine that?

As much as I hate to, I may have to change my ideas about who Beatrice really is.

The very thought gives me a headache. I hurry back into the store for the bicarbonate of soda.

I know I'm not supposed to ask adults personal questions, but Mr. Anderson never seems to mind when boys and girls come into his store. I guess it's because he has five children of his own. Just to settle things in my mind, I ask him a question I've been stewing over ever since I heard Shirley beg Beatrice for the thread.

"Mr. Anderson, sir? Is anybody allowed to buy things in this store?"

Mr. Anderson chuckles. "Now, Emily. Why would I turn away a paying customer?"

"So even if someone like Henry Jackson came in, you'd sell him what he was looking for?"

Mr. Anderson frowns. "I don't know anybody named

Henry Jackson. Is he new in town?" He measures some powder on a scale and scoops it into a glass bottle.

"No. He works for Papa as a blacksmith and has brown skin."

Mr. Anderson stops what he's doing and leans over the edge of the counter where I'm standing. He wrinkles his brow, looks at me, and says, "Is there somebody saying I don't allow Negroes in my store?"

I remember what Shirley said about Mrs. Peabody telling her she didn't belong here. "I...just wondered since I've never seen one here."

"Well now, I reckon there aren't any in this neighborhood. But you can tell Mr. Jackson and anyone else that they're always welcome here. Their money is as good as anybody else's."

"Thanks, Mr. Anderson." I smile at him as I pay for the bicarbonate of soda, relieved that not everyone is like Mrs. Peabody. I hurry down H Street toward Charlie's house, my head full of her nastiness.

Charlie is out running errands for his own mama. I give Mrs. Cook the jars of food from the basket and thank her for the butter, cream, and eggs. I have myself so worked up with worry about Shirley, Henry, Papa's business, and, Lord above, even Bea Pea. Carrying so much worry around without someone else knowing at least a part of it will eat a hole in me.

I run as fast as I can to the barn and into Papa's office. I set the basket down so hard, the eggs bounce into each other. "Papa," I gasp, working to catch my breath.

"I thought I sent you home."

"You did, Papa, but I have some worries."

"We can discuss your worries over supper. I have a lot of work to do getting this carriage ready for the president."

"That's part of my worry. Please, may I tell you?"

Papa sighs and puts down his pencil. "You have one minute."

I tell him about the Model T, Shirley, Beatrice, Henry, and the rest, my words spilling out in a rush, so I don't run out of time.

When I'm done, Papa says, "I know all about automobiles and Mr. Ford's Model T. There's nothing I can do about that. I also know there are only two automobiles in this part of Washington, DC. There are dozens of my carriages. Automobiles are just a toy for the rich. As far as Mrs. Peabody is concerned, how she handles her hired help is her own business. And just because Henry isn't working on this carriage, doesn't mean he won't be working on the next one."

"What about Beatrice?" I ask.

"How you feel about Beatrice is something you have to work out on your own."

"Did you know Mr. Anderson, the druggist, said Henry and anybody else with brown skin is welcome in his store?"

"That topic never came up in our discourse. But I always took him to be fair and a good judge of character. Now, get that basket to your mother right quick or I expect you'll have something else to worry about."

"So you're still going to make carriages?"

"As long as there's breath in my body."

"I sure am glad."

"Run along, Emily, so I can get back to this business you worry so much about."

I guess Papa is right about Mrs. Peabody. How she treats her hired help and daughter is her business. But it sure makes me glad for the kind of mama I've got.

If Mama thinks automobiles are foolishness and Papa thinks they are nothing to worry about, then I can save my worrying for Henry. That's about all the worrying I can handle right now, anyway.

When I pick up the basket, I see that two of the eggs have cracked open and made a sticky mess of the cream jars and butter. I guess now is one of those times I have a reason to worry about Mama. Why am I always making a mess of things?

I take out the broken shells and use my dress to wipe the sticky egg mess off the jars. Egg is oozing out of the cracks of the basket. I lick my finger and wipe the drips until there's no more yellow. Maybe Mama won't notice.

I sigh. Mama always notices.

There's nothing I can do about it now. I'll just have to take my punishment. I guess that's what happens when you worry too much. You forget to pay attention to some things because you're busy thinking about others.

CHAPTER 14

At first I'm not sure if I should tell Mama about the incident with the thread and what I heard regarding Mrs. Peabody, Shirley, and Beatrice. Then the more I think about it, the more I realize it might be good for Mama to find out what kind of person Mrs. Peabody really is. So after supper when the dishes are done and our bellies are full from the beef stew and corn bread, I tell her everything that took place on my errand.

She listens without interrupting and when I finish, says, "All the years I've known Mrs. Peabody, I've never heard her raise her voice to anyone. Maybe she was tired, frustrated, or a bit under the weather. She was at the druggist, after all. I know she's had difficulty finding reliable servants and had some things go missing in the past, things she was sure were taken by the help. Moreover, Emily, I don't think it's fair to judge a good Christian woman based on a conversation you shouldn't have been listening to in the first place."

"Yes, ma'am, but Shirley and Beatrice acted like they were afraid of Mrs. Peabody."

"Well now, you and I both know how Beatrice can sometimes dramatize things. She could have had other things on her mind. You know how you end up doing foolish things when you worry too much."

It's hard to imagine Beatrice worrying like me. What's she got to fret about? She has nice clothes, a fancy house, and more books and toys than anyone I know. Back when we were little girls — before she started her boasting and gossiping — I loved going to her house to play with all the wonderful toys she had. There were so many, she had a special room just for them.

"I'm sure Beatrice and her mama get along just fine. As for how Mrs. Peabody treats her hired help, that's really her business."

I frown. "That's what Papa said."

"I expect so. And I also expect you'd have a lot less to worry about if you spent your time minding your own affairs instead of eavesdropping on others." Mama brushes hair off my forehead and says, "Now clean up and get ready for bed."

"Yes, Mama." Mama may be right, but I know what I heard — even if I wasn't supposed to. It's awful hard to pretend it never happened.

Every year since I can remember, Charlie and I look forward to Halloween. Mr. Boggins, one of the farmers in town, has all the local children over to his place where we bob for apples, have hayrides in his big wagon, eat donuts, and drink hot apple cider. Then we have a parade to show off our costumes. We finish with a big bonfire while Mr. Boggins tells scary stories. That's always the best part, since he can make the hairs on your neck tingle with his tales about ghosts, witches, and haunted houses.

This is William's first year to celebrate with us, and I'm eager to share the fun with him.

But on Halloween morning, someone knocks at our door.

It's a brown-skinned boy, sweaty and out of breath from riding his bicycle.

"May I help you?" I ask.

"Who's there, Emily?" Mama sets down her dusting cloth and stands behind me at the door.

"Pardon, ma'am," the boy says to Mama. "I have an important message from Mrs. Jackson." He holds out a letter. "Is Mr. Soper here?"

"No, but I can take the message." She holds out her hand and sighs. "It's about Henry, isn't it?"

The boy nods. He gives Mama the letter.

"Thank you," she says.

He smiles and shuffles his feet, looking around like he's waiting for something.

"Oh . . . pardon me," Mama says. "Emily, fetch the penny jar from the cupboard."

I do what she asks, and Mama opens the jar, takes out some coins, and hands them to the waiting boy.

He tips his hat. "Thank you, ma'am." He pockets the

pennies and rides away.

"Why'd you give him money?" I ask.

"You always tip someone who provides a service or helps you in some way," Mama says.

I'll have to remember that the next time Mama asks me to do something.

She breaks the seal on the envelope and takes out the letter.

"What does it say, Mama?"

By the look on her face, I know it isn't good news.

Henry has gotten worse.

That afternoon, we pack a basket and ride out to see him. Mama even packs her medicinal elderberry brandy. She calls it nature's remedy for what ails you.

"I want to bring the horseshoe," I tell Mama as we're ready to leave.

"What on earth for? Henry has plenty of horseshoes."

"Not like this one." I push a chair up to the door. I use the prying end of Papa's hammer to pull the nails out.

"What is so special about this one?" Mama says as she fastens the buttons on William's coat.

"This one is filled with the spirit of the forge. Henry's spirit."

"Emily, I've never heard you speak such nonsense," Mama says.

I know it sounds foolish to think a silly thing like a horseshoe could hold a person's spirit. But when I touch the iron Henry took time to shape to his will, I feel the power and heat in it. Instead of a cold, lifeless hunk of metal, it is strength, hard work, and energy. As I squeeze the horseshoe, it nearly pulses in my hand. I suspect nobody but a blacksmith would understand it. Maybe if Henry holds it, he'll remember that feeling and get well.

This time, Mrs. Jackson greets Mama and me with a hug as we enter the house. We don't waste time with refreshments. Mrs. Jackson takes Papa to see Henry first thing.

Mrs. Jackson?" I say, "may I see Henry too?"

"Emily, mind your manners," Mama says. "You don't belong in there. You need to apologize to Mrs. Jackson."

"There's no need to apologize," Mrs. Jackson says.

"Mama . . . I have something for him, remember?"

"Emily, I don't want to hear any more of that foolishness."

Samuel, Joseph, and Alice shyly enter the room. Alice gives a small wave when she sees me. I hand her the basket of cider donuts, and Mrs. Jackson silently pinches off a piece for baby Abraham, sitting in his highchair.

As we stand in the crowded kitchen, I realize I have to make a decision. Do I behave as Mama expects me to, or do I try to convince Mrs. Jackson that I need to see Henry? The anxious faces of the children give me the courage to speak my mind.

I take the horseshoe from my coat pocket and hold it out to Mrs. Jackson.

"Please, Mama?" I wipe my eyes with the sleeve of my coat. I'm biting the inside of my cheek so hard, I taste blood.

Mrs. Jackson says, "Let her speak her mind, Ella."

When Mama looks at me, she is not pleased. I know I may be in for a big scolding later on. But for now she looks at Mrs. Jackson and quietly nods her head.

I explain about the horseshoe and how I think it's special. How if Henry can hold it and feel its strength and energy, he might get better.

I say it all through tears and when I'm done, Mrs. Jackson hands me a starched white hankie from her apron pocket. I wipe my eyes, blow my nose, and say, "Thank you, ma'am. Now may I please give this to Henry?"

She holds out her hand and I place the horseshoe in it. She stares at it a moment, all of us watching. Then she does something I've never seen a grown-up do. She presses it to her cheek, like I did when I picked it out of the box. That's when I know she understands.

Then she says, "Emily, I believe you're right. There is something different about this horseshoe." She hands it back to me. Mrs. Jackson and Mama lock eyes and say a whole bunch to each other without saying anything.

"Take it to Henry," Mrs. Jackson says. "Don't be long. He needs his rest."

When I enter the room, Papa is sitting on a chair next to the bed, his back to me, talking to Henry in his quiet, no-nonsense voice.

I listen, still as a statue. He talks about all the carriages they've made together. Some I've heard of, others must have happened before I knew about the magic of the barn.

Henry's eyes are open, but his breathing is fitful and ragged, like the wheezing of the wind through the cracks in the door during a storm. His sees me, and Papa turns around.

"What are you doing here, Emily?" Papa whispers.

I remember Mrs. Jackson telling me not to dawdle, so I come up to the bed and hold the horseshoe where Henry can see it.

I tell myself to be strong like the iron, so Henry won't see me cry. I say, "This is the horseshoe you let me choose from your box. It's a powerful one. If you hold it, I just know the spirit of it will help you get well."

I bite my bottom lip and watch Henry for any sign that he heard me.

"Emily, give that to me." Papa reaches for the horseshoe.

"No." Henry's voice is as soft and fragile as a snowflake. He looks at the horseshoe and nods his head so slightly, if I wasn't staring so hard, I would have missed it.

I lift the edge of the blanket to find Henry's hand. I feel the heat before I touch the skin.

"Oh, Papa, help me."

Papa places the horseshoe under Henry's hand and covers it again with the blanket.

Henry smiles weakly, lets out a rattly breath, and closes his eyes.

My heart races. "Oh Papa . . . he's not . . ." I can't stop the tears now. I tumble onto Papa's lap.

"He's resting, Emily." Papa lifts me into his arms like I was a baby. I bury my face into his shoulder so no one will hear me cry.

When I'm done, Papa dries my face with his handkerchief.

Mrs. Jackson enters the room.

"We were just coming out," Papa says.

Mrs. Jackson nods and looks over at Henry who still has a wisp of a smile on his face. "Thank you for coming." She bends down and kisses my forehead. "I will let you know when anything changes, Mr. Soper."

"Or if you need anything," Papa says.

"Yes." She places a wet cloth on Henry's forehead.

The ride home is quiet with all of us minding our own thoughts. Even William knows to be still. He contents himself with counting everything red that passes by.

I fall asleep thinking about Henry, hoping his horseshoe luck hasn't run out.

CHAPTER 15

Today is a big day. Election Day. It's the one day when men stop working and vote. Papa went to the Town Hall right after breakfast to cast his ballot. Mr. Taft is running against William Jennings Bryan. Mr. Bryan already lost two elections against President McKinley, and Papa thinks he'll lose this one as well.

He told Mama he was voting for Mr. Taft because Theodore Roosevelt thought he was the best man for the job. Mr. Roosevelt is a popular president who helped small businesses like Papa's, so his opinion on things carries a lot of weight as far as Papa is concerned.

We take a mock vote at school. Miss Carlisle talks about the work of the suffragists like Susan B. Anthony and Elizabeth Cady Stanton. Our teacher's eyes get sparkly and her voice rises when she tells us about this movement. I want to tell her that Charlie and I saw her the day of the rally, but Charlie thinks that would embarrass her. Miss Carlisle never once mentions it, so I suspect he may be right. At least in our pretend election, girls can vote, and when the ballots are counted, Mr. Taft wins by a landslide.

With Henry gone, I haven't had a chance to work on the model carriage I'm making for Papa. It's still in its hiding place under the canvas by the forge. I put one thin coat of paint on it, but it's just a shell without the iron frame and wheels.

Sam is extra busy with Henry gone, so I don't want to bother him asking for help. And I wouldn't give Mr. Martin the time of day, let alone tell him what I'm working on. He wouldn't approve anyway, and just the thought of him knowing about it would make the whole surprise seem tainted somehow.

Since Mr. Martin won't let me watch him at the forge, it's not as much fun to be in the barn. Papa has frown wrinkles most of the time. He doesn't say much. I know he worries about Henry and the president's carriage. It's been a week since the trip to Henry's house. There is no news. Mama thinks that's a good sign. I hope she's right.

I help Papa sort things once in a while, or I bring biscuits or cake for the men to have with their coffee. Mama had me bake the biscuits in another attempt to teach me proper lady-like ways. Mine came out a bit crumbly, but with Mama's jam they are passable. I also learn to scramble eggs and make lunch for me, Mama, and William.

"This is a nice treat," Mama says, eating my biscuits

and eggs. "It's rare when someone cooks a meal for me."

"I'm glad you like them, Mama." It surprises me that with all the fussing I do, I still look for ways to please her. Every time I please Mama — even when I don't try to — I get the nicest feeling. Like I could lift off the ground and fly.

"More eggs, Emmie," William says.

I smile and scoop some onto his plate, wondering where it all goes.

As if reading my thoughts, Mama says, "You eat enough for a boy twice your size."

William looks at Mama serious as can be and says, "Growing into a man takes lots of en-ger-nee."

"Energy," Mama corrects him, as we both laugh. It's especially funny since he says it with egg stuck to his chin and a dab of jam on his nose.

"Now that you're feeling a bit more confident in the kitchen, I'm thinking we should host the annual Ladies' Club Tea this year," Mama says.

I stop chewing in the middle of a biscuit bite. The Tea, as it is called, is a big to-do in the neighborhood. Ladies dress in their fanciest clothes and are waited on by their daughters, also dressed their best.

I attended my first Tea last year and didn't think I'd last to the end of it. There was so much worry about which knife spreads the clotted cream on the scones and which one is for the jam. How to use a napkin properly. Sipping tea without slurping and not putting too many lumps of sugar in the cup. It's one thing trying to mind my manners at home; it's another having to do it with so many ladies watching.

"Don't you think that would be lovely, Emily?"

"Lovely is not the word I was thinking of," I say. "Do we have to, Mama?" I set my fork down since I no longer feel hungry.

"It's a girl's duty to feel at ease and confident during such events."

"I never feel at ease having so many things to worry about."

"All the more reason to practice," Mama says. She looks at me across the table. "It may seem like torture now, but you'll thank me one day."

I doubt it. But there's no reason to tell Mama that.

"So then, we'll plan on hosting it the week before Thanksgiving. That gives us three weeks to plan the menu and send out invitations."

Mama's eyes get all glassy and faraway as she plans all the things she — we — will do to get ready. It all sounds like so much work. I get tired just listening to her, but I don't interrupt because if I stop her, she may decide to have me start some of the work now.

I take my plate to the sink. I look out the window and see a familiar wagon in the driveway.

When I open the door, there stands Charlie, his oldest sister Rose, and their daddy, Mr. Cook.

"Hello, Emily," Charlie says.

"Hi, Charlie. Hi, Rose. Hello, Mr. Cook, sir. Please come in."

Mr. Cook removes his hat as he walks through the door and greets Mama with a "Howdy, Ella."

Mama smiles and offers them seats. Out of Charlie's four sisters — Daisy, Iris, Holly and Rose — Rose is my favorite. She has eyes the color of cucumbers when they come fresh from the garden.

"Would you care for a drink or a biscuit and jam?" Mama asks.

"No thank you, Ella. We just finished our lunch," Mr. Cook says.

"Well then, what brings you here?" Mama asks. "If you're looking for John, he's in the barn."

"I have something to show John later on," Mr. Cook says. "I heard about Henry taking ill." He shakes his head. "How's the new smithy working out?"

"Fine, I guess." The look on Mama's face does not seem so certain.

I'm kicking Charlie under the table, itchy for the polite conversation to be over and anxious to know why they're here.

Charlie jabs Rose with an elbow, and they both grin at me like a couple of clowns. I can't help but grin back.

Mama clears her throat and shoots me a look that shouts, "Behave!"

"We're here to ask if we might take Emily on an outing with us," Mr. Cook says.

"What kind of outing?" Mama asks.

I'm so excited at the idea of going somewhere, it's easy to pay attention now.

"I'm taking Charlie and Rose downtown to the nickelodeon. The other girls are too young. Rose thought Emily might like to come."

"May I, Mama?" I am so pleased that Rose thought of me. Charlie always talks about the nickelodeon moving picture houses, and here was an opportunity to see one in person.

"Are you sure they're appropriate for children?"

Mama looks doubtful. She fears what Papa calls "newfangled things."

Even though I'm a little nervous about what to expect, my curiosity wins out over any worries.

Mr. Cook fingers his rust-colored beard and says, "Ella, you and I are like-minded when it comes to raising children. I wouldn't be taking my own if there was anything unseemly about it. It's a modern wonder, and I think Emily and Rose should witness it firsthand."

Rose and I lock eyes, too excited to say anything.

"Well, Harold, I leave Emily's well-being in your capable hands," Mama says.

So that's how I end up in the back of Mr. Cook's wagon with Rose and Charlie, a nickel in my coat pocket and my spirit overflowing with the thrill of a new adventure.

CHAPTER 16

We're bundled under wool blankets to keep most of the chill off. With a jug of hot chocolate and a sack of Mrs. Cook's sugar cookies, I hardly feel the cold.

Charlie does most of the talking, telling us about the things we'll see. He's been a couple times already, and since Rose and I are first timers, we nod our heads, nibble cookies, and listen. Charlie's excitement captures us like lightning bugs until we're glowing and buzzing with anticipation. Before I know it, we pull up in front of a store on Seventh Street. A huge sign in the window says: SEE THE WONDERS OF THE WORLD. HAVE SOME LAUGHS. ENJOY THE FINEST SONG AND DANCE ACTS AND MUCH MORE FOR ONLY 5 CENTS.

"Are we really going to see singing, dancing, and action all at once?" I ask. It's hard to imagine so many exciting things at the same time.

"Just wait until you see!" Charlie crows.

Mr. Cook ties up the horse and helps us all out of the wagon. "Bring the hot chocolate and cookies," he says.

"We can eat and drink while we watch the show," Charlie explains.

To say it is unlike anything I've ever seen only tells part of the story.

We enter a room nearly the size of the carriage barn. There are some benches up front, but they're taken. We sit in some straight-back chairs half-way down the room. No sooner do we sit than the lights dim, and a spotlight shines on the white wall in front of us. An enormous photograph fills up the light on the wall and starts to move.

It moves faster.

When a train moves past open fields, mountains, and lakes, I gasp. I can almost feel the wind on my face as the train rushes by. There are comedy skits with famous folks from vaudeville telling jokes, slipping on banana skins, and singing funny songs. I watch dance pictures, and one about the American Revolution with people dressed in costumes.

I'm dizzy, wide-eyed and breathless, watching it all. When I think it can't be any more exciting, a piano player begins music that starts out slow and easy. Once the action on the wall speeds up, the music does too, so I have the feeling I'm right in the middle of the fight between the cowboys and Indians. Then I'm chasing bank robbers down a city street. It's as if it's happening right now before us. Stories are told with signs spelling out what's happening, and, through it all, the piano music fills the room.

The sights make me want to jump from my seat, but the piano music makes me want to dance, soar, and fly. It's almost as good as being in the forge.

Almost — but not quite.

Still, I can't take my eyes off the piano player. In the dark it's hard to see what he looks like. His music makes the crowd laugh, cry, shout, and swoon, at just the right moments.

When it's over and the lights come back on, the piano player faces the crowd and takes a bow.

My mouth falls open and I can't stop staring at what I see.

A woman.

"Well, what do you think?" Charlie asks.

"I loved the song and dance parts," Rose says, smiling.

"Did you see the woman playing the piano? I didn't know girls could have such a job." I'm so excited I feel like it's my birthday and Mama made my favorite applesauce spice cake.

"It was a lady?" Charlie scratches his head.

Rose, Mr. Cook, and I all laugh at his confused expression.

"How could you not know that?" I say.

Charlie shrugs. "I was so caught up in the action, I didn't pay attention to anything else."

"She made the action," I say as we gather our coats and empty cups and head for the exit.

"You're crazy," says Charlie.

"What do you mean?" asks Rose.

"Do you think it would have been anywhere near as exciting to watch with no sound?" I say.

They all look at me, and Mr. Cook laughs and says, "By golly, Emily, that's something I never considered. The moving pictures were entertaining, but that piano told you when there was danger, or tragedy, or just plain fun."

"Exactly," I say. "What did you like best, Charlie?"

"The speeding train, when the pie hit the policeman in the face, the Indian fights." He laughs. "I guess I liked it all."

"How about you, Mr. Cook?" I ask.

Charlie's father smiles, scratches his beard, and says, "I reckon the part I like best is the idea that such a thing is possible. I'd love to examine the machine that makes it all happen. Sure is amazing to witness all this modern progress."

Mr. Cook is what Papa calls a tinkerer. When farm duties are over, he loves taking things apart to see how they work. He has even come up with better ways of doing things. He fixed his farm machines to run on steam so his horses can rest. He rigged up a sawhorse with a saddle and heavy springs so it bounces up and down when you sit on it, like you were on a real horse. Charlie's little sisters like to pretend they're cowgirls, and Will loves to ride on it when I bring him over there.

On the ride back, I think about what Mr. Cook said about progress. Even though I don't want things to change for Papa and his business, I am beginning to see that some changes are good. Like the piano player. No one minded that it was a woman.

"What do you want to be when you grow up?" I ask Rose and Charlie.

"I think I want to pilot one of those contraptions the Wright Brothers made," Charlie says.

"How can you make a living doing that?" Rose says what I am thinking.

"I haven't figured that out yet. But if I can't do that,

then I guess driving a train would be the next best thing."

"How about you, Rose?"

"I want to be a farmer's wife just like Mama."

That was just what I expected her to say. "Isn't there anything you want to do before you get married?" I ask.

Rose's face turns a pretty shade of pink when she nods her head and says, "I'd like to visit New York City."

"Oh," I say. Rose seems sorry she told me, so I smile to make her feel better. Still, I can't help wondering if I'm the only girl in the whole world who wants to be something besides a wife and mother. Why is it okay for boys to have bold and daring dreams, but girls are supposed to be content doing the same boring things their mamas do? If women like Miss Carlisle keep working for the right to vote, couldn't we be pilots, piano players, or blacksmiths if we wanted?

"What do you want to do when you grow up, Emily?" Rose asks.

"She wants to be a blacksmith," Charlie says.

Rose wrinkles her nose. "Girls aren't blacksmiths."

I sigh. Partly because I've heard that so many times, and partly because I know it's true. Now. But things are changing, aren't they?

"Until today, I thought I would try to be a blacksmith. But now that I know a woman can earn a living playing the piano like that lady in the nickelodeon, I might like to try that as well."

"Really?" Charlie grins.

"You don't think I could do it?"

"Oh, I know you could do it. The way you're always tapping out forge songs on your knees, all you'd have to do is tap them out onto the piano keyboard."

I smile, thinking of a new reason why I like Charlie.

Rose looks up shyly and admits, "I do have a secret wish that even Charlie doesn't know about."

"What is it?" I ask.

"To sing on the stage, in front of an audience."

"Like the choir on Sunday?" I ask.

Rose nods. "Except all by myself, with no one else singing."

"I could play the piano and you could sing. We'd be a duet," I say.

"That would be grand," Rose says.

I am so glad to hear that she has a real, fine urge to do something unexpected for a girl. We grin at each other.

Charlie pokes Rose in the ribs and says, "That's not a secret. I hear you singing all the time when you're in the privy and you think no one can hear." He hits a high note in an opera singer's voice.

Rose blushes and smacks Charlie on the arm. We have a hay fight, screeching and howling, until Mr. Cook tells us to pipe down.

Charlie raises his eyebrows and puts a hand over his mouth like he's suddenly remembered something. "Did Will ever find out that his mouse disappeared?"

I shake my head. With all the excitement about the parade, then worrying about Henry, I'd forgotten all about it.

"What mouse?" Rose asks.

Charlie tells Rose the story, ending with, "So you never talked to Will?"

"I forgot all about it until now."

"So when . . .?"

"We'll ask him when we get home," I say.

But once we're back, Mr. Cook rides the wagon to the carriage barn instead of the house.

"Why are we stopping here?" I ask.

"Daddy's got something to show Mr. Soper," Rose says.

"What is it?" I look at Rose and Charlie, who shrug.

We get to the barn door and bump into Mr. Martin on his way out. He carries a wooden box covered with a cloth. There's something about the box that draws my eyes right to it. Even with the cloth covering it, I can see a bit of the etched horseshoe Henry burned into the side. It's as familiar to me as my own name.

Mr. Martin nods to Mr. Cook.

"We're here to see Papa," I tell him.

"You just missed him," Mr. Martin tells Mr. Cook. "He went to the train station to pick up a tire shipment." He narrows his eyes at me and shifts the box under his arm. Little beads of sweat dance down his forehead. "Excuse me." He loads the box into the back of his wagon, unhitches his horse, and rides away.

"Well, I'll show this to your daddy some other time," Mr. Cook says. "Come along, kids. Your ma's probably wondering what's happened to us."

I drag my eyes away from Mr. Martin's disappearing wagon. "Can you come in the barn with me while I check something?" I ask.

"I don't feel right being in a man's business when he's not around," Mr. Cook says. "Something bothering you, Emily?"

All the excitement I felt from the nickelodeon is gone.

My chest feels tight and my head is pounding with the worst noise. "I think Mr. Martin just stole Henry's box of horseshoes."

"Really?" Charlie says. "How do you know? All he had was a big box."

I nod. "I'd recognize Henry's horseshoe box anywhere."

Mr. Cook sighs. "All right, Emily. Lead the way and we'll go look."

When we get inside, Sam greets us. "Emily and friends," he says. Mr. Cook introduces himself and they shake hands while my insides get so churned up, I feel the way cream must when it's on its way to being butter.

I take a deep breath. "Sam, may I check the forge a minute?"

He shakes his head. "Your daddy and Mr. Martin ain't here, and I don't feel right letting you in there."

Mr. Cook says, "Emily expressed concern that Mr. Martin may have taken something out of the forge."

Sam frowns. "What do you mean, taken something?"

"I'm just going to check." I push past everyone and rush to the forge.

"Come back here, Emily." I hear Mr. Cook and Sam, but I can't wait to explain it all. I have to see for myself.

I stumble through the gate that separates the forge from the rest of the barn, holding my breath. I rush to the corner where Henry keeps his box. A pile of horseshoes is there. BUT NO BOX. I sift through them, counting. It's only when I reach forty-four that I let out my breath and feel the weight lift from my chest.

Well," Sam asks, "anything missing?"

"The horseshoes are here," I say, looking around.

"The box is gone."

"Why would Mr. Martin take an empty box?"

Sam scratches his head. "I saw the box Mr. Martin had under his arm. That the one you mean?"

I nod.

"Well, Emily. I don't see how you can be sure it was Henry's. It looks like all the other boxes we got around here. You come out of there now."

Were the horseshoes in the box the day Henry got sick? I can't remember. I take one more look around the forge. The fire simmers, bellows next to it. The anvils and hammers are at rest. A couple of wheels lean against the rail. Everything seems to be in order.

Yet it doesn't feel right.

If Mr. Martin had just any old box, why did he try to hide it when he saw me? A plain old wooden box is nothing to hide.

Unless there was something in it.

Were those beads of sweat on his forehead from the forge or from something else? Despite everyone's belief all is well, I leave the barn with a feeling of dread.

Chapter 17

At supper that night, Mama and Papa are full of questions about the nickelodeon.

"It was fine," I say. I pick at a chicken leg, pull a piece of meat off, and shove it in my mouth.

"Use a fork, Emily," Mama says.

I take my fork, stab the leg, lift it to my mouth, and bite off a piece.

Mama sighs. "That's not what I meant."

"What's wrong, Emily?" Papa asks. "You are usually quite a chatterbox. Not still fretting over Henry, Mrs. Peabody, and the rest, are you?"

"No. I mean, I am worried about Henry, but I've decided to pay no attention to what Mrs. Peabody says or does." I wonder if I should tell about my funny feelings regarding Mr. Martin.

It's important to do what is right, even if it means making some folks — like my parents — angry. While I'm not in the mood for a lecture on proper behavior, I'd feel much worse if my feelings about Mr. Martin ended up being right, and I'd said nothing.

"Emily Soper!" Mama only uses my full name when she's mad or upset. "You were bursting with excitement when Mr. Cook took you out this morning. What happened to all that enthusiasm?" She looks at Papa. "Did you have an argument with Charlie or Rose?"

"No, Mama," I say. "It has nothing to do with the nickelodeon. That part of the day was wonderful. I promise, I will tell you about it." I sigh, blowing so hard, the water in my glass quivers.

"Well then," Papa says, "If it's not Henry, Mrs. Peabody, or your adventure today, what are you worried about?"

"I have a funny feeling about Mr. Martin." There, I've said it.

Papa sets down his fork. "What kind of feeling?"

I tell them about our stop at the barn on the way back from town. How Mr. Martin had the box covered and seemed in a hurry to leave. I even mention how Mr. Cook and Sam didn't want me in the forge, so they don't get in trouble. When I finish, Papa is quiet a minute, like he's digesting more than chicken and turnip greens.

"You say you counted the horseshoes and they were all there?"

I nod.

"Nothing else was missing?"

"It didn't look like it."

"Sam didn't notice anything wrong?"

"No."

Mama frowns at Papa. "Do you have reason to suspect Mr. Martin of wrongdoing, John?"

"He's been a decent worker so far. Never says much. Keeps to himself. Arthur Peabody gave him a hearty recommendation. Says he's done good work for him in the past."

"Beatrice's father?" Remembering his comment at the suffragist rally, I make a sour face. William giggles and blows raspberries across the table at me. He thinks it's a game, but I couldn't be more serious.

"Emily Soper." Mama says my full name again. "I know you're not fond of Beatrice, but Mr. and Mrs. Peabody are good Christians and law-abiding citizens."

I remind Mama about how Mrs. Peabody acted toward Shirley and Beatrice.

Mama sighs and shakes her head. "We talked about that before. I don't condone harsh treatment of another human being regardless of who they are or what they've done. But I'm sure Mrs. Peabody has a good reason for her behavior. We shouldn't judge her based on one incident."

I'm weary from trying to convince Mama that Mrs. Peabody may not be who she appears to be. So, I put all my energy into a sigh and let it pass. For now.

"So," Papa says. "All this may be about nothing, but I will keep an eye on Mr. Martin all the same."

I brighten a bit. "Thanks, Papa."

"Feel better?" Mama asks.

I nod.

"Then tell about the money," William says.

"What money, Will?"

"You went in the wagon with Charlie and Rose to see money."

I laugh when I realize what he means.

"The nickelodeon has nothing to do with money," I say. I hold up my fingers like six-shooters. "Just things like cowboys and Indians, cops and robbers, song and dance, and men acting like clowns. Pow, pow." I shoot my imaginary guns in the air like Annie Oakley.

William's eyes are like wagon wheels as I tell my story. I save the best part for last.

"The piano player was a woman, Mama, and she was proficient and thrilling to listen to."

"Good piano players usually are," Papa says.

"Do you think . . ." I look back and forth between Mama and Papa, a smile creeping onto my face that I can't hold back. "Do you think I could learn to play the piano?"

Mama's face lights up and a sparkle shines in her eyes.

"I think that's a wonderful idea," she says. "We'll start lessons right away."

Mama is as good as her word.

After school on Monday, I have my first piano lesson. The Reverend and Mrs. Porter's daughter, Claudia — who is also the church organist — gives piano lessons to anyone who wants to learn. Mama says her fee is very reasonable.

Claudia is what Mama calls an old maid since she's twenty-five and unmarried. Claudia is so thin, she looks like she could take off like a kite in a strong wind. She's got big brown eyes with lashes like Colonel, except Claudia's always blink like she's not sure if she wants them to be opened or closed. When I look at her too long, I start blinking too.

Miss Porter — that's what she wants me to call her when she's working — has me start my lessons with something called scales. We do them up and down the piano keys. By the end of the lesson, I can do them with my eyes closed. It's not nearly as exciting to hear as the nickelodeon piano player. But I figure she probably did scales when she was my age.

Claudia — I mean, Miss Porter — tells Mama I'm a natural talent at the piano. Mama is pleased.

Not nearly as pleased as I am.

As much as I've always longed to be a blacksmith, I know in my heart it's terribly hard work and requires the strength of an ox — or a big, muscular man — to be good at it.

But being a nickelodeon piano player seems like a fine and daring occupation for anyone, boy or girl. I already feel like I have the rhythm for it, thanks to so many of Henry's songs stored in my head. The very idea of bringing those songs out sends the most delicious shiver down my spine.

Maybe if I'm brave enough like Miss Carlisle and the nickelodeon player, I can make my own dreams come true. For the first time in ages, I'm thrilled to be a girl. That's a really good feeling.

CHAPTER 18

There has been no news regarding Henry's condition. Mama says that's a good thing since it means he hasn't gotten worse. I still worry. How could someone be ill in bed for more than a month? When I get a cold and have to lie down for a day or two, I'm beside myself from being so cooped up. Poor Henry must feel like he's in prison without seeing the sun or feeling fresh air on his skin. I say a little prayer every night hoping he'll be up and about real soon. Lately I've added a second prayer, asking for a tea party without any disasters. I hope that's not asking for too much.

The dreaded Tea is only three days away.

Our kitchen looks like one of those fancy downtown stores where lacy curtains are on display. This is due to Mama airing out the best linen table covers and napkins. They began their airing outdoors until it started to rain. Now they hang on ropes across the kitchen. Mama nearly had my hide when I tried to hang them over the stove, thinking they'd dry quicker. "And turn black with soot in the process." Mama frowned. "Honestly, Emily, you should know that."

"Yes, ma'am." I've been yes ma'aming all week in an effort to be as agreeable as I can. It's given me a headache and a sour stomach.

One exciting new thing entered our lives. At least William and I think it's exceptional. Mama decided to try a breakfast that didn't have to be cooked. She bought this new product called Corn Flakes that comes in a box. Without milk, they crackled like autumn leaves, adding a new sound to our quiet mornings. Mama had us pour milk on them to reduce the noise. Either way, it freed her from stoking up the stove to cook eggs, oatmeal, or grits first thing in the morning. She says it's a blessing on wash day when she heats up all the water and feels like she never leaves the kitchen stove.

Mama and I sit down one night after supper to decide what to serve for the Tea.

"Let's serve the Corn Flakes. Then we won't have to cook anything."

"That is not proper food for a tea," Mama says. She looks at me and smiles. "I do like the idea of not doing much cooking. We can have simple sandwiches like egg salad, chopped ham, and butter and jam. How does that sound?"

"Like too much work." I wiggle my eyebrows at William, who giggles and tries to wink at me. He ends up closing both eyes at the same time. We trade silly faces until Mama says, "And there will be no foolishness now or at the party."

"Yes, ma'am." I wink at William one last time.

"Emily Soper."

I show her my serious face.

"You know how important this tea is. You won't do anything to disgrace this family." Mama's not asking.

It hurts me to think she doubts my ability to be a proper hostess. I try to remove the worry crinkles from her forehead when I say, "Mama, just because I'm not fond of domestic things doesn't mean I won't try hard to please you." I look at her, hoping she realizes I mean what I say.

"I'm doing this for your benefit," she says.

I sigh. "I know, Mama." To make amends I say, "Can we make some of Mrs. Jackson's gingerbread?"

"Excellent idea. I've been meaning to try that recipe using vinegar. We'll make some scones with clotted cream as well." She opens the cupboard. "With this tin of shortbread, that takes care of dessert."

"Are we done?" I am anxious to get out to the barn and see how the carriage is coming along. I get fidgety and blue being away from the forge too long. Even though Mr. Martin won't let me watch, I still enjoy the sounds and smells from a distance. If Papa isn't around, maybe I can put a second coat of paint on my model carriage. I haven't touched it in ages.

"Let's review seating arrangements. There will be eight, counting you and me. We can all fit comfortably around the dining-room table."

"Who's coming?" I know Mama invited Beatrice and Mrs. Peabody, because Beatrice mentioned it at school. When I tried to ask her how Shirley liked the thread, Beatrice told me to mind my own business. When has she ever done that?

"Besides the Peabodys, there will be Mrs. Porter and Claudia, Miss Carlisle, and Mrs. Coopersmith."

"Who's Mrs. Coopersmith?"

"She's the new president of the Ladies Club. Her husband is the manager of the bank where Papa does his business."

"What about Mrs. Cook and Rose?" I ask.

Mama sighs. "Elvira doesn't care much for teas. Even when we were girls, she'd stop playing when I suggested we have a tea party."

Sometimes I think Mama ended up with the wrong daughter. Or maybe I ended up with the wrong Mama. It would be nice if there was something we could agree on.

So, except for Beatrice and Claudia, it will be a room full of old hens cackling and clucking at each other, showing off their fancy feathers. When I think about it, Beatrice fits into that group, old or not. I make a promise to myself to be polite and respectful to Mrs. Peabody and Beatrice for Mama's sake.

I wish for it all to be over, but I know that's a wish that is wasted.

Mama decides to move my usual Saturday night bath to Friday so I can be sweet smelling and shiny for the Tea. I haul out the washtub from under the sink and fill it up with water that's been heating on the stove. When it's about half full, I strip off everything except my underclothes and climb into the tub.

Instead of the usual Naptha soap, Mama hands me a bar of her special lavender-scented soap. I rub it over my cotton chemise until I get some suds. Mama helps with my back. She scrubs my hair until my scalp tingles and I holler in protest. Then I slip off the chemise and soak in the suds. The warm, soapy water slides over my skin like fancy silk. The smell of lavender makes me wish for summer. I'd stay in the tub until it got cold, but William has to have his turn.

I wrap myself in a towel, and after putting on clean nightclothes, I sit while Mama tortures my hair with a comb, trying to work out the tangles. When she gets tired of my squirming and hollering, she rubs a little mineral oil on the comb to help it slide through. I go to bed feeling pampered and content, like a spoiled cat.

I would have slept like a cat too, if it hadn't been for Mama's scream.

Chapter 19

I jump out of bed so fast, you'd think my bloomers were on fire. I've heard Mama holler before, but I've never heard her scream.

I follow the horrible sound to Will's room and as soon as I go in, I get a funny feeling in the bottom of my belly. Will's sobbing and Mama's waving a hankie like a flag of surrender.

The hankie with the scorched iron mark on it.

The hankie that held the dead mouse.

"Why on earth would you keep a dead mouse?" Mama asks Will. "In your bed, no less." Mama looks down at her feet at the blackened, stiff mouse. She kicks it and sends it sliding across the floor toward the door.

Right where I stand.

I shiver at the sight of that poor, shriveled carcass.

Will's crying so hard, he can't even talk.

He sees me and sobs, "Emmie, tell M-Mama it's not d-d-died." His little red face is covered in snot and he shakes so hard, I hear his teeth chatter like a rattle.

I squeeze my eyes shut at his pitiful request, my shame getting the best of me.

"Do you know something about this?" Mama asks me in disbelief.

What has my little white lie done to poor Will? There's nothing to do now but tell him — and Mama — the truth.

I sit down on the bed next to Will. I reach out to touch him, and he jumps into my lap like a puppy, waiting to be soothed. I caress his soft hair.

"I'm sorry, Will," I say. "I shouldn't have let you believe the mouse was only sleeping."

Mama sighs. She looks at both of us and says, "Suppose you tell me the whole story from the beginning."

I tell her how Will rescued the mouse from the mouth of a cat and wanted to keep it as a pet. How I didn't have the heart to tell him it was dead, so I let him think it was sleeping. I explain how I'd convinced him to put the mouse where he found it so its mama could come back for it.

"A few days later, I looked in the spot where we buried it and it was gone. I figured an animal came and got it. I meant to ask Will about it, but I forgot."

Will is quiet now, so I ask him, "Why did you dig it up?"

He sniffs. "In my dream, a fox came and stole Mousie. So when I woke up, I brought him in so he wouldn't get stoled." He sits up and looks at Mama. "I was just going to keep him until I saw his mama. I tried to feed him bread crumbs." Will wipes his eyes on his arm and shakes his head. "He wouldn't eat."

"And why do you suppose he wouldn't eat?" Mama asks.

Will shrugs.

Mama waits for me to explain this to Will.

"The first time you found Mousie, he was already dead. You know what dead means, don't you?"

Will frowns. "It means he's never going to wake up?"

"That's right."

Will's eyes fill up with tears, like he's ready to cry all over again. "I didn't mean to kill him." He sobs.

"Dear God," Mama says. She takes Will into her arms and rocks him.

All this time, he thought he was the one who killed the mouse? How could I have been so careless and stupid! "You didn't kill him, Will," I hurry to reassure him. "The mean old cat did when she tried to eat him."

"She did?" Will sniffs and rubs his watery eyes.

I nod.

"I'm glad the cat did it," Will says.

"Why?" It's a shock to hear him say that, especially after all his carrying on.

"Cats are supposed to kill mouses. Boys aren't."

As long as I live, I don't expect I'll ever have a heart or brain as large as his. My chest swells just knowing he's my brother.

"You're amazing," I tell him.

He nods, which makes Mama and me smile.

We sit there a minute, listening to Will's breathing calm down.

"Well," Mama says. "I think that's enough excitement for one night." She tucks the covers around Will and kisses him on the forehead.

"I'm going to bury Mousie now, okay?" I kiss Will on his rosy cheek.

"Put him under Mama's roses. He likes that spot." Will yawns, curls up under the blanket, and closes his eyes.

Mama shakes her head and whispers, "Wrap it back up in this hankie, and I'll have Papa bury it when he gets in."

It takes me a long time to fall asleep. When I do my dreams are filled with dead mice, mysterious boxes, and Henry.

Chapter 20

Tea Day is bright and sunny. If it weren't for the November cold, I could pretend it was summer, since the smell of lavender is still in my hair.

Papa is taking William out for the day so Mama doesn't have to worry about him being underfoot. They are going to the Smithsonian Museum after first visiting Henry. We made extra tea sandwiches for Papa to take along. I watch them ride away in our covered carriage and long to be with them.

"Emily, help set the table before our guests arrive."

I sigh and drag myself away from the window.

We put out Mama's best china plates, saucers, and teacups. Normally, we only use them on Thanksgiving and Christmas, another sign this isn't a regular day. I help Mama polish the silverware and tea service so it shines. Crisp napkins are next to each plate, the same rosy pink color as the tablecloth. Mama even cut some green pine sprigs and holly to dress up the center of the table. I like it, but tell her a red ribbon would add nice color, so she digs a piece of red cloth from her scrap basket and ties it in a fancy bow. I'm pleased that she likes my decorating suggestion.

I put sugar lumps into the polished silver bowl and set a spoon inside. With pewter candlesticks, the table is something to see. We set out a three-tiered plate with the gingerbread, scones, and shortbread squares. We spread egg salad on brown bread, ham on white, and butter and jam on small biscuits.

Everything is ready.

Mama is so pleased with my help, she lets me pick who I can sit next to. I set myself between Miss Carlisle and Claudia, on the opposite end from Beatrice. If I have to make tea-party conversation, at least it will be with people I like.

I get a last-minute inspection from Mama. My light blue satin dress is so fancy, I'm afraid to move in it. If I get any tea or jam on it — well, I don't want to think about that. I try to reason with Mama about wearing one of my school dresses, but she says no. Her only daughter is not going to look ordinary hosting her first Tea.

Mama is a vision in Alice Blue satin. The president's daughter Alice Roosevelt made the color popular, and the blue-green shade is perfect for Mama's blue-green eyes.

Her brown hair is piled around her head like a fuzzy halo, fastened with a feathery satin bow. With a bow in my hair as well, we look like we belong together. When Mama looks at me, her eyes tear up. "You look so grown up, and you've worked so hard! I'm proud of you, Emily."

"Thank you, Mama." I kiss her cheek. Her warm praise gives me the confidence I need to get through the day.

Still, by the time our visitors arrive, butterflies have taken over my stomach and are looking for a way out. I drink water to settle my insides and then help Mama greet our guests. Miss Carlisle arrives with Mrs. Peabody and Beatrice. I remember the promise I made to myself and use my best manners to greet them. I take their coats and place them carefully on the sofa in the parlor like Mama said. By the time I get back to the group, Mrs. Porter and Claudia arrive, and then Mrs. Coopersmith. With all coats removed, and greetings done, I get a chance to take in the sight of so much satin, lace, and feathers.

Mrs. Peabody wears a maroon dress. Her corset reminds me of a dam holding back the floodwaters. It's a wonder that she can breathe with everything pulled so tight. Her face is flushed, matching the feathers on her dinner-plate-sized hat. Her ever-present fan flaps at the air like a wing. Beatrice wears pink with rabbit-fur cuffs on the sleeves of her dress. Poor bunny.

"You look absolutely charming, Emily," Mrs. Peabody says.

"Thank you, ma'am," I say, even though her compliment is as syrupy and fake as Beatrice's smile.

"How nice of you to have us to Tea." Mrs. Peabody's eyes search the dining room, not missing a thing. "Lovely table, Ella."

"Thank you, Agnes." Mama smiles graciously.

Beatrice, who seems to be attached to her mama's side, gushes about the greenery to Mama and sends one of her pretend smiles my way. I pretend smile back.

"Please have a seat," Mama tells our guests. I made place cards with my fanciest handwriting so everyone knows where to sit.

Mrs. Porter and Claudia wear blue dresses with hats to match, looking almost like sisters instead of mother and daughter. Mrs. Coopersmith, the banker's wife, wears a necklace with so many gems, when the candlelight catches it she blinks her eyes from the glare. Her hat is so full of feathers, you might think a bird was sitting on it.

Our last guest, my teacher Miss Carlisle, is plain in comparison to all the fur, feathers, and lace surrounding her. She wears a gray silk dress and a simple bow tied in her hair. Except for Mama, she's the prettiest one here.

When everyone is seated, Mama looks at me so I know it's time to pour the tea. Mama passes a sandwich platter around the table as I get the teapot from the sideboard. Pour from the guest's right side, Mama said. I take a deep breath to calm my hostess jitters.

I start with Miss Carlisle.

"Claudia tells me that Emily began piano lessons." Mrs. Porter begins the tea-party conversation.

"Yes, she has," Mama says.

"She's a quick learner." Claudia nods.

Miss Carlisle smiles when I finish pouring. I move to Mrs. Coopersmith.

"Beatrice has been playing for nearly two years now," Mrs. Peabody announces.

"Who do you take lessons with?" Claudia asks Beatrice.

"A professor at the Music Conservatory," Beatrice boasts.

"They are known for training the best," Mrs. Coopersmith says. "Thank you, dear," she adds when I finish pouring her tea. "Many have gone on to orchestra positions."

I glance at Claudia, whose eyes blink even faster than usual.

"I really enjoy my lessons with Clau — I mean Miss Porter," I say.

Claudia smiles at me and resumes her normal eye blinking.

I pour Mrs. Porter's tea.

"Emily tells me her father is making a carriage for President Roosevelt," Miss Carlisle says as she places an egg sandwich on her plate and passes the rest to Mama.

"Oh, yes," Mrs. Peabody gushes. "Beatrice told me about that. How is the new blacksmith, Mr. Martin, working out?"

I smile at Beatrice as I get ready to pour her tea. She puts a hand by her mouth, blocking her mama's view, and sticks her tongue out. Makes me wonder why I ever felt sorry for her.

I pour Beatrice's tea all the way to the top of the cup so when she puts milk in it, it will spill over into her saucer. She frowns at me, but I don't care. I would stick my tongue out at her, but I don't want to upset Mama.

"Mr. Martin seems to be a good worker," Mama admits.

"He's worked for us in the past," Mrs. Peabody bellows. "We only hire the best."

Mrs. Coopersmith puts three lumps of sugar in her tea and murmurs, "I wasn't aware John hired a new blacksmith. What happened to the old one?"

"Henry is sick," I mumble. I place the empty teapot

on the sideboard, pleased that I poured without any mishaps. I pick up the second pot of tea.

"Henry's been ill for quite a while," Mama explains. "It happened right after John got the order for the carriage. He didn't know what he was going to do without a blacksmith. To have an order from the president and not be able to fill it is unacceptable."

"Of course," agrees Mrs. Porter.

All the ladies nod politely.

I pour Claudia's tea. She thanks me and places a jam biscuit on her plate.

"Well, I happen to know for a fact that they aren't very dependable," Mrs. Peabody says. "They just can't be trusted." She puts a ham sandwich on her plate.

"What do you mean, Mrs. Peabody?" Miss Carlisle asks.

I smile at Miss Carlisle, grateful she asked the question bubbling in my mouth.

Mrs. Peabody favors Miss Carlisle with a smile. "Well, dear, I'm sure Mrs. Porter and Mrs. Coopersmith will agree with me when I say this, since their granddaddies had to deal with these people as slaves, just as my granddaddy did."

"Well . . ." Mrs. Porter hesitates. "I . . ."

"I would rather not —" begins Mrs. Coopersmith before Mrs. Peabody interrupts.

"Ladies, you know as well as I do that sneakiness is part of their makeup."

Mama clears her throat to get my attention. She wants me to finish pouring tea. There's only Mrs. Peabody, Mama, and me left to pour for.

But Mrs. Peabody keeps talking as if she's forgotten there is anyone else in the room.

The more she talks, the more my insides shake.

I bite my tongue to keep from disgracing Mama by speaking out of turn.

"Colored folks need to be watched carefully or they'll steal everything they can get their hands on. They must be ruled with a firm hand. Really, Ella, I can't let my maid out of my sight for a minute. They're best left to work with their own kind. If I could find a white maid, I'd hire her on the spot. It saves so much trouble in the long run. Don't you agree?" Mrs. Peabody looks at Mrs. Porter and Mrs. Coopersmith.

They dab their mouths with their napkins and look everywhere except at Mrs. Peabody.

Mama's face is red and her eyes flash.

Mrs. Peabody keeps talking, and as I look around the table, it's like everyone's mouth has been glued shut.

Doesn't anyone have anything to say in Henry's defense?

"You're wrong . . ." I begin until Mama practically shouts.

"Emily, please pour the tea!"

Only then does Mrs. Peabody stop talking. Everyone lets out a breath of air at the same time.

I've bitten my tongue so hard, I can taste blood.

I lift up the teapot and move to Mrs. Peabody's side.

Hands shaking, I do the only thing I can think of. I tip the pot, spilling tea all over Mrs. Peabody's lap.

"Emily!" Mama yells.

"You clumsy brat!" Mrs. Peabody jumps up from her seat, shoves the teapot from my hand, and sends it crashing to the floor. Beatrice screams. Mama springs from her seat. She hands Mrs. Peabody her napkin.

"You did that on purpose, you little beast," Mrs. Peabody shouts. There is so much hatred in her eyes and voice, a chill courses through my body.

I run from the room, my feet feeling as heavy as my heart.

The last thing I hear is Mama calling my name as I run out the door into the cold afternoon air.

CHAPTER 21

I run to the carriage barn, tears streaming down my face. Cold air burns my wet cheeks. My dress catches on a bramble bush. I yank it free, ripping a gash in the silky fabric.

"Shoot!" I scream into the air. I've broken my promise and disgraced Mama. I feel worse than I've ever felt. Why shouldn't my dress be as torn and shredded as I feel?

I reach the barn and throw myself at the door. I try the handle. Locked. Papa went out with William. Was that this morning? It feels like forever has gone by since then. I rub the snot off my nose with the sleeve of my dress and bang on the door, even though I know no one will answer.

I run to one side of the barn. I pound at the windows that are shut tight and scream until my throat is raw. I stumble over stones and lumps of coal piled up for use in the forge, stomping my way to the other side where one window is opened a crack. I force it up as high as it will go and squeeze through, tearing another strip off my dress.

I land in a pile of sawdust and wood shavings, in Sam's part of the barn. I lay there, spilling out my misery in a waterfall of tears.

I hate Mrs. Peabody for what she thinks about colored people in general and Henry in particular. I hate Mama for expecting me to be proper. Is that more important than speaking up when you think something is wrong? I hate everyone else at the Tea for their silence.

Most of all, I hate myself for not stopping Mrs. Peabody sooner. If I had poured her tea first and kept her eating, she would have been too busy to say such awful things. If I was braver I would have told her to shut up, even if it made Mama angry.

I hate Papa for not being here. I hate Henry for being sick. All the hate makes me cry until I have no tears left. I close my eyes, counting my sobs like they are sheep.

Crash!

The sound of breaking glass.

My eyes snap open. Am I dreaming?

What's broken? Why do I smell smoke?

I stand up and run across the room onto the main floor of the barn.

"No!" I scream at the sight of a flaming torch inside the president's half-built carriage.

Inches from the wall of the barn.

Jagged bits of broken glass cover the floor. Smoke

stings my eyes and bites at my throat, making me cough. I spit out a gray glob onto the floor.

I scream as another torch sails through the broken window. It lands on a pile of scrap wood. The fiery torch licks the dry wood, sending sparks and smoke into the air.

I run in search of the water bucket. It always stands at the railing next to the forge. I remember putting it there myself.

It's gone.

Why would Papa move the bucket? How can I put out the flames?

Think.

Everything here is made of wood.

A gust of air blows through the broken window, fanning the flames. The two fires send out tongues of orange heat, singeing the wall. More smoke fills the room.

The carriage has caught fire.

I can't see anything.

Except the floor.

I get down on my knees and suck in a breath of air to clear my head.

What can I use?

Horseshoes?

I scramble like a bug across the floor to the forge, ignoring the jabs of pain on my knees and legs from the broken glass.

The horseshoes are still in a pile on the floor. How can I carry them all?

I pull my ruined dress over my head. I pile the horseshoes onto the dress and drag the heap back to the fire.

I dump the pile of iron onto the burning carriage bed.

Hissss. A black cloud of choking smoke makes me gag and sends me back down to the floor.

How will I put out the second fire?

"Emily!"

"Papa!" I feel like I screamed the name, but it only comes out in a croaky whisper. "I'm on the floor," I whisper-yell. I lay a cheek on the floor, searching for Papa's feet.

My head feels heavy. It's so hard to breathe. I want to close my eyes and go to sleep.

"Emily, where are you?"

I try to tell Papa, but my voice is gone.

I force out a moan. I crawl until I hit a wall. Can't go anymore.

The wall moves. It reaches for me. Takes me into its arms.

"It's all right, Emily. Papa's here."

I open my burning eyes.

Papa looks like a stagecoach bandit with a bandana covering his mouth and nose. He rushes from the barn, holding me tight. I bury my face in his neck, smelling shaving lotion mixed with sweat. So much better than smoke.

No more worries.

The cold air slices through my flimsy chemise and bloomers. It slaps my skin with goose bumps and I can't stop shivering. Papa wraps me in a blanket and sets me down on a crate next to Mama. She gives me a cup of water.

Everything happens in a blur of motion.

Shouts. People rushing about.

William with Miss Carlisle. Charlie. Mr. Cook. Someone sitting on the ground.

I shiver and my eyes water. I wipe them with the edge

of the blanket. When my head clears and I'm breathing better, I start to make sense of things.

Charlie and Papa run back and forth to the broken window with milk cans. They dump the contents onto the torches. I hear the sizzle and smell the burnt milk. They refill the empty cans with pump water. Mama and Miss Carlisle fill buckets with water as well.

William sits under a tree on an overturned crate. He sends me a small, shy wave.

Mama fusses over me, smoothing my hair and adjusting the blanket. She lets out a hissing sound at the sight of my bloody shins.

"Stop, Mama. I'm all right."

"Thank the Lord and your papa for that. Be still while I get the glass bits out of your skin."

She squeezes warm, soapy water over the cuts, picking out pieces of broken glass and dirt with a long pair of tweezers. A splinter is usually enough to make me fuss, but my whole body is so numb I barely feel the poking.

Then I see Mr. Martin sitting on the ground with his back against a tree. Mr. Cook is pointing a shotgun right at the middle of his chest.

CHAPTER 22

Why is Mr. Cook holding a shotgun at. . . ? What did Mr. Martin...?

I can't put into words the awful thoughts in my head.

It's only when I see a police wagon pull into the drive that I realize the terrible truth.

Mr. Martin tried to burn down Papa's barn.

I shiver and wrap the wool blanket tighter around me. I feel like I'm about to throw up.

Did Mr. Martin know I was in the barn?

Mama puts her lips on my forehead. "No fever," she says. "You look so pale." She wraps a second blanket over my bandaged legs.

"Why did Mr. Martin try to burn down the barn?" I croak. I take a sip of water, but it doesn't make my throat feel any better.

Mama sighs. "I don't know."

Papa comes over to me, looking me up and down as if some of my parts might be missing. His face and the bald spot on his head are covered in sooty sweat from all the smoke.

"I'm okay, Papa. Why did Mr. Martin. . . ?"

"Everything will be sorted out when I get back from the police station," Papa says. He puts a hand on my shoulder and kisses my forehead.

He and Mr. Cook follow the two police officers as they escort Mr. Martin away with his wrists tied behind him and a hateful scowl on his face.

Charlie runs over to us and says, "We put both fires out. How did you get the idea to throw the horseshoes over the torch?"

"I couldn't find the water bucket."

Charlie nods. "Mr. Martin dumped it and left it outside. I think that was part of his plan. Anyhow, the cold horseshoes smothered one flame, so we were able to work on the other one."

"Really?"

Charlie frowns. "You don't look too pleased."

I shiver and let out a slow, tired breath. "My head is fuzzy with everything that happened since the Tea. . . " I bite my lip and look at Mama and Miss Carlisle, who is now standing next to her.

Mama's eyes are red, like she's been crying. Shame washes over me like muddy water. I made Mama cry because of what I did.

"Mama." I reach out to her and she hugs me close, stroking my head with her warm hand. I break away and say,

"I'm sorry I ruined the Tea and destroyed my dress. I'm sorry I embarrassed you." I look at Miss Carlisle. "You too, Miss Carlisle."

"There's no need to apologize, Emily," Miss Carlisle says. "Your actions saved your daddy's barn."

Mama takes my hand and says, "Emily Soper, if there's anyone who should be ashamed, it's me."

I stare at her, surprised. "What did you do, Mama?"

She shakes her head. "It's not what I did. It's what I didn't do. I was so concerned with having you learn to serve a proper tea, I failed to set an example when it came to righting a wrong."

"I should have spoken up when Mrs. Peabody said those terrible things," Miss Carlisle says. "I think I was in shock."

"We all were," Mama says.

I breathe in a deep, heavy breath, trying to understand all this. "You're not mad that I dumped tea on Mrs. Peabody?"

"Your method was a bit harsh, but she deserved it," Miss Carlisle says.

"Yes, she did," Mama agrees. "I should have been the one to do it." She frowns. "I owe you another apology. You warned me about Mrs. Peabody and I wouldn't listen." Mama wipes her eyes with a soiled hankie.

"You're not angry at me, Mama?"

"I am very upset that you ran away, but the rest. . ."

Mama squeezes my hand and looks at me like she's found something she'd lost.

The heavy, sad feeling that was pressing on me eases up a bit. I drink the last of the water in my cup and say, "What happened when I left?"

"Let's get back to the house and I'll tell you the story," Mama says.

CHAPTER 23

We gather in the parlor, where the air is still warm from the fireplace embers. Mama turns up the gas lamps as we settle onto the settee. Charlie has Will on his shoulders. They're watching me as if they expect me to perform feats of wonder. I'm too tired to do anything more than wrap the blanket tighter around my shoulders as Mama begins her story.

"After you ran from the Tea, I told the guests to leave. Mrs. Peabody fussed about her ruined dress, saying if you were her child, you would be severely punished. Beatrice tried to calm her mother. I think Beatrice was embarrassed at the way her mother behaved." Mama shakes her head. "Beatrice wanted to help look for you. But Mrs. Peabody was so angry."

Mama bites her lip and looks at Miss Carlisle who says, "Mrs. Peabody slapped Beatrice across the face and just about dragged her out the door."

I put a hand over my mouth. The shock of it sends chills through my body.

Poor Beatrice. No wonder she acts like a different person around her mama.

"When the guests left, Miss Carlisle and I began a frantic search for you. We checked the barn, but when we found it locked, didn't look further. We went to Charlie's house, to see if you'd gone there. Mr. Cook and Charlie took us in their carriage to search for you and to fetch Papa."

"Oh, Mama. I'm sorry you had to look everywhere for me." I lift her hand onto my cheek. It upsets Mama to tell the story even with me here safe. How upset was she when she couldn't find me?

Miss Carlisle adds her part of the story.

"I was very disturbed by Mrs. Peabody's behavior, but unable to do anything. You may not know she allows me to live rent-free on a small cottage on her property, so I felt in an awkward position. When you dumped the tea, however, I knew I had to do what I thought was right, regardless of the consequences. So I did not return home with her."

Miss Carlisle smiles. "Mrs. Peabody was not pleased. But that didn't bother me like I thought it would."

"Does it bother you now?" I ask.

"No, and that's thanks to you and your bravery."

"I didn't feel brave. Only mad."

"Still, it made us all examine what we are made of." Miss Carlisle's pretty face wrinkles in disgust and maybe embarrassment.

I think back to the suffragist rally and how much courage Miss Carlisle showed then. "I never doubted your fine character, Miss Carlisle," I say.

"Thank you, Emily. It means a great deal to know that." She squeezes my hand.

"Where will you live, Miss Carlisle?"

"Until I find a permanent solution, I'll stay with my aunt in Alexandria. It will mean a train ride each morning and evening, but I can manage that."

I wonder if now is the right time to ask her about women voting, but just then Papa and Mr. Cook come bursting through the front door, back from the police station.

"How's the little firefighter?" Mr. Cook asks as he removes his coat and settles into the rocking chair.

"Except for a froggy voice, she's all right," Charlie says. He dumps William from his shoulders onto the empty overstuffed chair.

Papa sits next to me on the settee and takes my hand in his. He looks at me over the top of his glasses. "It was foolish and dangerous for you to stay in that barn."

"But Papa . . ."

He holds up a finger. "Terribly foolish and dangerous. And also very brave. You saved the barn from serious damage. One wall has to come down and part of the floor. It'll take a few weeks before we can get the materials to fix it."

"And the president's carriage?"

Papa shakes his head. "I'm afraid we'll have to start all over again. The iron-work is sound, but all the wood was singed and smoke damaged."

"Oh, Papa."

He dismisses my concern with a shake of his head. "Small potatoes when I think of what could have happened.

We'll have a lot of catching up to do, but it'll get done."

"Papa, how did you know where I was?"

"Mr. Cook found me at the Smithsonian as William and I were leaving. When they told me what had happened, I knew you had to be in the barn. There was nowhere else you would go."

Papa knows me so well.

"We got to the barn just as Mr. Martin threw the second torch through the broken window." Papa takes a hankie from his pocket and wipes his forehead. He squeezes my hand and continues.

"He was ready to toss in a bucket of sawdust when Mr. Cook wrestled him to the ground and held him still with the shotgun." Papa looks at Mr. Cook. "He'd have gotten away for sure if you weren't so quick."

Mr. Cook strokes his rusty beard. "The thought of Emily being in there . . . " He wipes his eyes with a huge fist. "I've got daughters of my own."

Everyone grows quiet thinking about that.

"So while Mr. Cook stopped Mr. Martin, you came into the barn," I say to Papa.

"Yes." Now it's Papa's turn to wipe his eyes with a fist. "Smoke and flames and you were nowhere to be seen. Those were the longest seconds of my life, until you crawled up against my leg."

"I was on the floor because it was the only place where I could breathe and see a bit."

"Good thinking." Papa smiles and kisses my forehead gently.

"My hero!" I climb onto Papa's lap and wrap my arms

around his neck.

"I'm not a hero, Emily. Just a grateful father, lucky to have his daughter safe and sound."

"Amen to that," Mr. Cook agrees.

"But you knew where to find me."

"If you hadn't run to the barn, I wouldn't have come home early or opened it until tomorrow morning. Who knows what kind of disaster might have occurred."

I think about that as I hug Papa tighter. "What's going to happen to Mr. Martin?"

"He'll be in jail awhile, I suspect," Mr. Cook says.

"I'm glad." Everyone must think the same thing since I don't get scolded for being disrespectful.

"Why did he do it, Papa?"

"Charlie and I wondered the same thing." Mr. Cook shakes his head, bewildered.

"I'm not sure if I've got it all figured out myself," Papa admits. "I think we should hear the good news first. Henry is recovered and feeling much better."

"Thank the Lord!" Mama cheers.

This news has me feeling lightheaded, almost dizzy. I can tell that Papa — and everyone else — feels the same way by the looks on their faces. We all seem to take a deep, slow breath at the same time. A shared sigh of relief.

I listen to Papa finish his story.

"After visiting Henry, I went to see Mr. Martin," Papa continues. "I told him his services were no longer needed since Henry will return to work this week."

That news sends me flying. I jump off the sofa and twirl in circles around the parlor. "Did you hear, everyone?

Henry's coming back."

"We heard," everyone choruses, and Charlie spins William around like a top.

I stop twirling, suddenly serious. "So Mr. Martin was mad about losing his job and that's why he tried to burn down the barn?"

"Not exactly. He knew when I hired him he was filling in until Henry came back. That shouldn't have made him do what he did."

Mama, Miss Carlisle, and Charlie look as confused as I am.

"What was it then, John?" Mama asks.

Papa looks at all of us. His eyes stop on Miss Carlisle. "I'm glad you are here for this. Maybe it will be useful in a class lesson. It's unpleasant listening though," he says.

Miss Carlisle nods.

"Mr. Martin, like Mrs. Peabody and some other folks, didn't like a Negro working for me. Mr. Martin belongs to a group of white supremacist people who think whites should only work with other whites and leave colored folks with their own kind. He figured burning down the barn would put me out of business and end Henry's employment as well."

"Oh, John." Mama's face is pale and she looks like she might cry.

"What kind of lesson does that teach our young?" Mr. Cook shakes his head in disgust.

Miss Carlisle says, "To think he might have killed an innocent child because of that hatred. Mr. Lincoln must be rolling over in his grave with grief to think that after all these years since the war, people still act this way. The war was supposed to change things."

There's that word again. Change. Even after a horrible war, people still hold on to their old ideas about folks like Henry. The truth of it makes my insides churn and ache.

Maybe folks can do without physical changes like cars and electricity. But old ideas about colored people and women should change. They must.

A shiver goes through me and I want to cry all over again when I think of how proud I am to be surrounded by people who welcome that kind of change.

"Emily, you were also right about something being taken from the forge," Papa says.

"She was?" Charlie sounds surprised.

Mr. Cook and Papa nod in unison. "I found a box full of Henry's tools in the back of Mr. Martin's wagon," says Mr. Cook.

"I knew it!" Mr. Martin had been a rotten egg from the moment I laid eyes on him.

"Found something else too." Papa nods to Mr. Cook who steps out of the room and returns with something wrapped in canvas.

My heart somersaults into my throat when I realize it's the model carriage I am making for Papa. "That was a surprise . . . Henry was helping . . . Why did Mr. Martin . . . ?" I sigh in frustration and heartache, unable to complete my thoughts.

Papa lifts out the unfinished carriage. "You did this yourself, Emily?"

I nod, biting my lip to keep from crying. With all that's happened, having my surprise revealed because of Mr. Martin's behavior is almost more than I can bear.

"How did you manage this without my knowledge?" Papa doesn't say it with anger or surprise, but rather a kind of awe. That gives me the courage to speak again. "I had to work when you weren't around. Which wasn't easy. Henry hid it for me between visits. We even found a way for me to hammer the iron away from the fire." I blow out so much air, I feel like a deflated balloon. "All for nothing. The surprise is ruined." If Mr. Martin were here, I could spit in his face and not even feel bad about it.

"The surprise may be ruined, but I will none the less look forward to seeing the finished product," Papa declares.

I gasp. "You mean I can still work on it?"

"I don't see why not. You and Henry invested a lot of time in it already."

"And I haven't finished painting it, so you won't know the color or how I'm going to decorate it." I brighten a bit knowing that at least that will be a surprise.

"Now," says Papa, "there's only one thing left to do before we eat what is left of your tea sandwiches."

"What?" I ask.

He takes something out of his trouser pocket and holds it up. A horseshoe.

"Is that Henry's horseshoe?" I reach for it.

Papa places it in my hand. "Henry returned it. Now that he's well, he no longer needs its luck. He thought we might."

Henry's right. I rest the horseshoe against my cheek while Papa gets a hammer and nails.

Legs wobbly from exhaustion and happiness, I stand on the chair as Papa hands me the hammer. Everyone watches as I put the horseshoe back where it belongs.

Mr. Cook and Charlie leave, but Miss Carlisle stays for a bite to eat.

We sit down to a late Saturday supper of stale sandwiches, dried-out gingerbread, and cold tea. I've never tasted anything so delicious.

"Will you still be able to get the president's carriage ready on time, Papa?"

"Yes, I will. There is a lot of work to do, but we'll hang up some canvas until the wall gets replaced. Can't hold up the job just because a wall's missing."

"Hooray! Papa, Sam, and Henry will be making carriages forever!" I cheer.

Papa sighs and looks at Mama. His face is wrinkled and worry-crinkled. He must be tired from being a hero.

I smile and look at the horseshoe hanging above the door again. The horseshoe luck is back. With Henry in the forge where he belongs, Mr. Martin in jail, and Papa finishing the carriage for President Roosevelt, everything seems to be working out just the way I want it.

CHAPTER 24

Thanksgiving is quiet this year, but after all that has happened, I'm glad. We have a welcome-back celebration for Henry the day after. I make a banner from a strip of canvas with the words WELCOME BACK HENRY. Papa hangs it over the doorway so everyone sees it when they enter. Mama even lets me bring Will in to see it and share some of the refreshments we prepared. Warm apple cider with sugar cookies that I baked myself. Mama doesn't like to make cookies because it takes too much time, what with rolling the dough and cutting it into shapes with a knife or biscuit cutter. She says it's easier to dump batter in a pan for cake.

I follow a recipe in her Boston Cooking-School Cook Book and use a knife to cut heart-shaped cookies from the dough. It takes a while, and I stay by the stove every minute so the cookies won't burn. In the end, it's worth all the work.

They come out of the oven all golden brown. Sprinkled with cinnamon and sugar, they taste like heaven.

I like knowing that I can do something on my own and have it turn out well. It makes me change my mind a bit about domestic things. I can see how a lady could get a special feeling cooking or baking something that people enjoy. Mama raves about the taste, which gives me a happy feeling. As if I've just popped out of the oven myself, all warm and heart shaped.

I can tell Henry is excited about the party because he can't stop smiling.

"Y'all didn't need to make a fuss over me," he says. "It feels like it's my birthday."

"It almost is," I tell him. "Since you're good as new after being so sick."

"That's a good way to look at things, Miss Emily." He eats another one of my cookies. "These are mighty tasty. You have a fine hand for bakin'."

I can feel my face get warm from the compliment. "Thank you," I say as I pass the plate to Papa, Sam, and Will, who's sitting on Papa's knee. It's wonderful to see Papa so relaxed here in the barn, since he's usually rushing around and busy.

Just when I think I can't be any happier, Henry looks at Sam and asks, "Ready?"

Sam nods and takes out a harmonica from his pocket. Henry has two spoons held between his fingers so that the backs are touching. While Sam blows out "Oh Susannah" on the harmonica, Henry taps the spoons on his knee.

Who would have thought you could make music with spoons? I grab Will and spin him around, while Papa taps his feet in time to the song. Has there ever been a better way to celebrate than having people I love all together enjoying themselves?

I beg for another tune, but Papa says it's time to go back to work.

It's thrilling to be back in the barn hearing the familiar song of the forge. Henry is thinner, but his eyes shine like a new piece of coal. He has me pick out another horseshoe to hang over the barn door. The wall is still missing, but a heavy canvas curtain keeps out most of the chill. And nothing seems to have affected the spirit of the place. I still get the same warm, tingly feeling being here.

"This here's a special place, and I hear we're lucky it's still standin'," Henry says.

"I'm glad you're back, Henry,"

"Me too, Miss Emily. Thanks for the cookies. You are a natural-born baker, that's for sure." He eats the last one before taking a piece of iron from the fire.

I take a satisfying breath when he begins his hammering music.

"How do you like your new hammer?" I ask.

"It's a mighty nice one. Works fine too." Henry chuckles. "It'll take a while to break in so it feels like mine."

Even though Papa recovered all of Henry's tools, he bought Henry a new hammer as a welcome-back present.

"Emily, Mama wants you and Will back home," Papa says. "Tell her not to hold supper. We're working as long as we can tonight." He gives Will a hug and kisses my cheek.

"Can I come back to the barn again, Papa?" Will asks.

"We'll see. Run along now."

Wanting this wonderful feeling to last, I suggest, "Will,

let's hold hands and skip back to the house."

His eyes light up and he says, "I'm a good skipper. Watch."

As we head back to the house, my smile is as wide and full as a lucky horseshoe. Everything is just the way I want it.

I knew it was too good to be real. When I think things are going to stay as I want them to, change comes along and messes everything up.

Beatrice isn't at school anymore. Her mama put her in a private school in Georgetown. Since she doesn't go to our church, I don't see much of her. I thought I would be glad, but I never got to ask her how she felt about what I did to her mama or about the slap. Miss Carlisle said that Beatrice cried and carried on when Miss Carlisle left. For once, I might have liked to hear what Beatrice had to say. I know now I was wrong about what kind of person she really is.

Miss Carlisle tells me something even worse. Something so hurtful, I can't bring myself to tell Papa.

She says that before she left Mrs. Peabody's house, she overheard Mrs. P telling a group of her lady friends that Papa's carriages were inferior and a poor investment. She told them they should tell all their friends and neighbors to spend their money elsewhere.

I ask Mama why people spread lies about other folks, hoping it will ease my hurt without actually telling her what Mrs. P said.

"Emily, spreading lies makes some people feel better about themselves."

"It's mean, and I bet if God is listening to the lies, he would be angry," I say.

"Yes, he probably would," Mama agrees.

Sometimes grown-ups sure don't act grownup.

Charlie follows me around like a chick after a mother hen, always asking me to retell the Tea events. You'd think he would get tired of hearing about it. Instead, he's taken to calling it the DC Tea Party and says it should be in the history books right next to the famous one that happened in Boston.

But it doesn't feel like history when Mama says I have to stop my piano lessons.

"Right now we have so many other things that require money," Mama explains. "All the new materials to fix the carriage and the barn repairs. Once Papa gets paid for this carriage and gets a few more orders, we'll be back on our feet. It's only temporary."

I can tell by the sad, sorry look on Mama's face that she feels just as bad as I do.

A thought pops into my head and I say, "Maybe I can sell some of my cookies to pay for the lessons."

"And what money would you use to buy all the ingredients?"

I guess I didn't think it all the way through. I'll have to come up with another plan or I'll never learn all the things I need to know to be a successful nickelodeon player.

The biggest changes are the way Mama and Papa treat me.

If I thought Mama was watchful before the fire, since then she's anxious and smothering, reluctant to take her eyes off me for fear I'll disappear. She's always asking me where I'm going, even if it's only to the privy. She expects me to spend every minute trapped in the house, where she hovers over me like a mother duck protecting her fledgling. I have to beg to visit the barn, and when I get there, Papa is so busy checking on me, he can't get his work done. No matter how many times I say, "I'm okay, Papa, what could possibly happen to me here with you, Sam, and Henry?" he just sighs and tells me to go home.

Then, at times when Mama and Papa think I'm out of hearing, they talk in hushed voices that are filled with sounds of worry and upset. As soon as I enter the room, their words stop, but their faces can't hide the things that bother them.

You would think they'd be celebrating now that Mr. Roosevelt's carriage is nearly done.

CHAPTER 25

Night after night for weeks, Mama keeps Papa's supper warm so he can finish the carriage for the president on schedule. One day, when I know it's close to being done, I head out to the barn.

Papa hurries by on my way in. He has so many ropes, tapes measures, half-full buckets, and fabric swatches hanging on his arms and around his neck, he looks like one of those traveling salesmen who hawk their wares through the streets of town.

I skip after him. "Will Mr. Roosevelt pick up the carriage? Can I sit in the carriage? Will you meet Mr. Roosevelt?"

"Too many questions," Papa says.

"But, Papa . . ." His usual stare silences me.

"It wouldn't do to have you mess up the carriage of the president," he says.

"Papa, I would never!" I smooth out my dress, standing taller.

Papa's mouth twitches in an almost-smile. "You want to ride in this carriage?"

He hears my heart's biggest wish. "Yes!"

"Then go home and help Mama take care of William."

I pretend to leave, but hide where he can't see me. I hear Papa talk to Sam and Henry in his crinkled-brow voice.

"Only one more to build after this. I'm not sure what we'll do. The lumber is coming in this week for the barn repair, but with the weather so cold, I don't expect to get much of that work done. Been making carriages all my life. After all we've been through to build this carriage, I should have been working on a plan to keep this business going."

What does Papa mean?

"I know there's folks that don't like me workin' here," says Henry. "I wouldn't blame you, Mr. Soper, if you ask me to leave. A man has got to do what he can to provide for his family."

"It wouldn't be worth running this place without you and Sam, Henry. Although you might have a better opportunity of steady employment elsewhere. I wouldn't hold you back if you needed to move on."

Is Henry going to leave?

There's a long stretch of silence.

Finally, Henry says, "No, sir. You stood by me when I got sick. I still got some work on the side. I'll be okay."

"I appreciate that," Papa says. "How about you, Sam?"

"I like working here, and I have a bit put away for lean times like this. I'm not going to leave just because things have slowed some." Sam pauses, then adds, "I don't know which makes me madder, that rat Frederick Martin or automobiles. One or the other will be the ruin of us."

Do motorcars put the worry in Papa's voice and the crinkles on his face? Do they mean the end of this wonderful place? Surely folks still need carriages. Not everybody can be ignorant enough to believe Mrs. Peabody.

If Papa gives up now, then Mr. Martin wins.

I can't let that happen. I won't let that happen.

The president still wants a carriage. Wait until he sees his carriage. If he likes it, others will too. The proof is in the pudding, as Mama says.

CHAPTER 26

When carriage delivery day comes, I'm like a balloon, one puff away from bursting. I wear my Sunday dress. Is velvet and lace special enough for something so beautiful?

The glossy blue-black finish glistens like the feathers of grackles. My finger skates along the blue striping that took weeks to dry. There is a silver-handled door on each side, polished to such a shine, I can see my reflection in it. A small glass window in the rear and three movable windows around the front and sides have fancy cloth pulls that can be pulled down for privacy. A special cover on the doors keeps mud from being thrown up by the wheels. Two lamps are attached to each side of the body near the front window.

Papa spreads a blanket over my legs and feet. It's the same soft blue wool as the carriage seat. I take a deep breath and am rewarded with all the smells I love — wool, varnish, paint, and new wood. Such a glorious perfume!

Papa climbs onto the driver's seat, protected by an apron that can be used as a lap cover during bad weather. Even though it's a pleasant day, Papa places the apron over his lap. I bet he feels like royalty just being able to drive this wonderful creation.

He looks at me through the front window.

"Ready?"

"Giddy-up!" I shout through the talking tube. It's for the president to speak through to his driver, the gadget that Mr. Cook wanted to show Papa the day we came back from the nickelodeon. Papa thought it was a dandy idea for this important carriage. This Brougham is larger than the one Papa usually makes. It takes two horses to pull it.

Papa taps Colonel and one of Mr. Cook's horses named Scout, and off we go to the White House stables on Seventeenth Street.

No clickety-clacking on the cobblestone streets. The hard rubber tires, wooden wheels, and strong springs make this carriage glide like a sleigh on ice. I feel like Cinderella riding in her magic coach. I close my eyes and pretend Mr. Roosevelt is with me. I ask how he likes the carriage. He says it's fit for a king. Too soon Papa pulls up to the stables.

Two men are waiting for us. They don't look like the picture of Mr. Roosevelt I saw in the newspaper.

They come up to greet us. Papa winks and says, "This is Emily, my carriage tester."

The taller man with a mustache says, "What's the word on this carriage, Emily?"

"It's fit for a king," I say. It's hard to stand still, I'm

that excited. "That's what I'm telling Mr. Roosevelt."

Mr. Mustache says, "The president is too busy for carriage business."

"But this is Papa's best carriage!" How could the president not be here to greet Papa?

"Emily, mind your manners." Papa's eyes scold as well as his voice.

Too busy? Papa wasn't too busy to bring the carriage himself. He could have sent Sam. If I have to mind my manners, what about Mr. Roosevelt? Shouldn't he say thank you for Papa's hard work? If he knew all that Papa went through to make this carriage, surely he would want to shake his hand.

While the men talk, I slip inside the stables. Maybe Mr. Roosevelt is busy with his horses. Taking care of horses is hard work, and Mr. Roosevelt loves horses.

A horse whinny-whispers. Tails swish hello. Sweet hay and horse smells welcome me. Beautiful horses, with names above their stalls. "Renown," "Georgia," "Gray Dawn," and a pony named "Algonquin."

Algonquin winks at me. I reach out to stroke his muzzle. He kicks the stall. I scream, stumble, and fall in a pile of hay.

Papa rushes in, the men close behind.

"Trouble?" Mr. Mustache says. "You shouldn't be in here, young lady."

"The pony kicked and . . ." I am more shamed by the look on Papa's face than by the fall.

"What are you doing in here?" Papa asks.

"I wanted to tell Mr. Roosevelt . . . "

Papa takes my hand and pulls me up. "Apologize to these gentlemen."

"I'm sorry, sirs." I squeeze my eyes shut, hoping that when I open them, the look on Papa's face will be different.

Mr. Mustache says, "No harm done, young lady."

I open my eyes. Papa shakes hands with the men and we leave the barn. Papa's look cuts through me like Mama's butcher knife.

"I'm disappointed, Emily."

"I wanted Mr. Roosevelt to meet you, so I could tell him how hard you worked on the carriage. What a great job you did."

Papa shakes his head. "No one has to tell me I've done a good job. The work is my reward. I thought you knew that, Emily."

It seems like I don't know anything anymore.

"Is the president's job more important than yours, Papa?"

"Emily, the president looks after the whole country. I do my best to take care of you, your brother, and Mama."

I know what I think, but there's no more discussion. Papa lifts me side-saddle onto Colonel and then climbs onto Scout. He holds both harnesses as the horses trot toward home.

I can't even enjoy the rare opportunity to ride on Colonel by myself because Papa is so quiet, it hurts my ears. The trip home seems much longer than the one in the carriage.

CHAPTER 27

It's been a week since we delivered Mr. Roosevelt's carriage. After what I did at the stables, Papa barely talks to me. I don't know if I'll ever get to finish my own carriage. But that worry is at the bottom of all my others. Papa won't let me into the barn. He's given me that punishment before, especially when Charlie and I have gotten into trouble. But this time it worries me for many reasons.

First, because since the DC Tea Party, Papa has stopped teaching me new words. I thought maybe he ran out of them until I heard him tell Mama they needed to find a proper avocation for me. The only reason I found out it meant job was because Mama said she was running out of proper jobs for a young lady.

My second worry is from listening to Papa agree with Mama when she said I am too old to spend time in the barn.

How could they think such a thing? Didn't they say I was the one who saved the barn? That's like me telling Papa he can't be with me anymore because he saved me from the fire. It's a conundrum for sure.

Then there's one worry that's the worst of all.

Papa told Mama he might have to close the barn and find a new avocation. Just the idea of that makes my insides boil and shiver at the same time. The boiling comes from the fact that if Papa closes the barn, Mr. Martin — and people who think and behave like him — will be victorious, and nothing will have changed. The shiver is from the loss of all the wonderful things that happen in the carriage barn.

Even though Papa doesn't realize it, he could use my help. No one cares about the carriage barn and the magic that happens there as much as I do.

Today I'm going to the White House. Miss Carlisle says ordinary folks can meet the president by showing up at the north door. So that's what I'm going to do. I ask Charlie to come with me, but he has to go right home after school to help Mr. Cook bale the last of the hay from the field and chop all the fallen logs for firewood.

So I'm on my own.

I cross First Street, following the route Papa took along Pennsylvania Avenue when we delivered the carriage. Carts, coaches, wagons, and two motorcars rumble past. I shake a fist at the automobiles. How dare they worry Papa with their noisy engines and foul the air with their smelly gusts of smoke!

Cold wind snaps at me like an angry dog. Too many people are on the sidewalk. I hop onto the street to go faster.

I scream as an ice wagon misses me by inches.

The driver swerves, splashes mud, and yells, "Watch where you're going!" I jump onto the curb, miss it, and tumble into the dirty street. A man in a wagon asks if I need help. I dismiss him with a wave of my hand, too humiliated and embarrassed to accept any kindness.

Waiting for my heart to quiet, I examine myself to see what damage I've done. A torn stocking, muddied coat, scraped knee, and wounded pride. I wipe my eyes on my coat sleeve, and pick myself up. Maybe I don't look proper enough to be a White House visitor, but I'm going anyway.

When I finally get to the White House, a sign on the door says visiting hours are over.

It can't be. Not when I'm this close.

I jiggle the door handle. It's locked.

What should I do now? It's a long way back. I've never been out this far from home after dark.

I don't feel so bold anymore. I remember how upset Mama and Papa were when they couldn't find me the day of the Tea.

If I had told them my plan, they never would have let me go. But now that I'm here, cold and alone, I wish I had told Henry or Sam.

Papa can't come for me because he doesn't know I'm here. How come every time I try to help, it only causes trouble and misery? Why do I let my worries wipe away my good sense?

I sit down on the step, because I don't know what else to do. If I stay here, I'll be frozen and dead by morning. I hate myself for being so foolish.

Then I remember.

There's one place close by that's safe and warm. Hay makes a good bed. I get up and walk to the stables a few blocks away on Seventeenth Street.

A boy is saddling a horse outside the stables.

"Who are you?" he asks, before I can ask him the same thing.

"Emily Soper, the carriage maker's daughter. I came to meet President Roosevelt."

"He's not here."

"I know. It's a long way home. I thought I could rest here."

"Where do you live?" the boy asks.

"H Street, near the train station."

"I'll take you home," he offers.

"I can't ride with strangers," I say. He's older than me, but not yet a man. He's long and lean like Charlie, with a head full of golden-brown hair the color of honey. Would Mama think this boy was a stranger, with his prominent cheekbones and crooked, friendly smile? It's the kind of smile that suggests a bit of mischief could be in store.

"I'm Archie Roosevelt." He offers me his hand to shake.

My heart knocks at my chest, like a horse kicking a stall. "Do you know President Roosevelt?"

"He's my father." Archie grins.

My stomach somersaults. "Are you teasing?"

"Do you think just anybody can take out this horse?"

I shake my head. "Your papa lets you ride by yourself?"

"I'm fifteen and have been riding since I could walk. I even have my own pony."

"Algonquin?"

Archie looks at me. "How do you know his name?"

I tell him about my first visit here and how I peeked in the stables.

Archie's smile gets bigger, like he enjoys the naughtiness of my story.

"Your father made the new carriage?"

I nod. "Isn't it grand?"

"She's a beauty, all right. So, Emily Soper, do you want a ride or don't you?"

"I do. Will we ride Algonquin?" I ask.

Archie shakes his head. "Too small for the two of us. We'll take Gray Dawn here." He gives the horse a loving pat as he secures the saddle.

While Archie works on saddling Gray Dawn, I take in details of the barn I missed the first time I was here. With the exception of its grand size and brick castle-like exterior, the smells of leather, oats, and sweet hay are the same as Colonel's barn. This one has lots of windows and is lit by electricity. It even has a telephone! I wonder how many people it takes to keep the stables so neat. Our barn seems to always need tidying.

"Ready?" Archie asks.

"Oh, yes," I say.

He helps me into the saddle, climbing on behind me.

I hold tight to the saddle horn as my knight urges on the galloping horse, swift and bold.

"Loosen up your hold," Archie says. "Your knuckles are turning white."

I loosen my grip a little. I can't help smiling, thinking that Charlie will never believe this.

Archie handles the horse like he's ridden forever.

Cold air stings my cheeks and hands, but I don't care. It's thrilling to be sitting on a horse with the president's son. Besides being a competent horseman, Archie is strong and handsome. It's like a dream, sitting close enough to feel his breath on my face. If I was the kind of girl who boasts and brags — like Beatrice — this would be a story any girl would envy.

We leave carriages, and even a motorcar, in the dust as Archie brings me to the tree-lined edges of town. As fast as ice cream melts on a sunny day, I am home, just as the crescent moon replaces the sun.

"Thank you," I say, as Archie helps me down from the horse.

He waves, tips his hat, and rears up the horse before disappearing like a Rough Rider swallowed by the night. Farewell, Prince Charming. I sigh.

Mama is peering out the window as I walk up the drive. She flies out the door, grabs me in her arms. She hugs me so hard I feel like a big foot in a small shoe.

"I'm okay, Mama."

Now there are angry eyes with words to match. "Emily Soper, where were you? Why were you out alone? How did you get home? How could you do something like this? Papa is searching everywhere for you!"

"I was trying to help Papa," I say before she asks more questions I don't want to answer.

Mama shakes her head. "How can you call it help when you cause trouble and worry?"

She won't let me be until I confess everything. The only part I leave out is the ride home with Archie. It's the one good thing that came from my misadventure and I don't want it spoiled by Mama's disapproval.

She sends me to my room without supper. It's just as well because I don't feel like eating. My heart is like a heavy stone. I am sick, tired, and disgusted with myself for being a worry and a trouble. And I didn't even get to talk to Mr. Roosevelt.

I press my nose to the window, staring into the darkness.

Where is Papa?

When I think I can't stand waiting anymore, he trudges across the yard, a lantern lighting his way. Did I put the stoop in his shoulders? Did I take the bounce from his step?

I hurry down the stairs and run out to him. "Papa, I didn't mean to be late."

He falls to his knees, arms held out.

"I went to talk to Mr. Roosevelt." I wipe the tear on his cheek.

Papa takes off his glasses, wipes his eyes, and shakes his head. "How can I keep you safe when you do foolish things? From now on, you come straight home from school. No more carriage barn, and no more talk about Mr. Roosevelt."

It's a punishment I accept without complaint.

CHAPTER 28

At school the next day, Charlie asks if I got to meet the president.

"No, but I met his son Archie! I was so cold and tired that I went to the stables to rest, and Archie was there. He gave me a ride home."

I can tell Charlie's excited by this part of the story because his face lights up like the lantern Papa uses to walk home from the barn at night.

"What's he like?" Charlie asks.

"He's friendly and kind. You'd like him, Charlie. He seems like the sort of boy who enjoys a good adventure."

"Boy, I wish I could have gone with you. I've heard a lot about the president's sons and all the things they do at the White House. Did you know President Roosevelt lets his children slide down the banisters?"

"Papa says they sometimes roller skate inside the White House too." I say. "Can you imagine that? Mama has a fit if I even run through the house."

We both spend a quiet moment imagining life at the White House.

"It's not as much fun as gliding down a banister, but do you want to come over and help me build a doll house for my sisters for Christmas?"

"I would like to very much, but I can't." I tell him about my punishment. From very little freedom, it feels like I'm being restricted to no freedom at all.

Papa is so upset with me, he has Sam take me back and forth to school, walking all the way. I can't ride in a carriage. I ask Papa if I can do chores. Sweep floors. I even remind him about finishing the model carriage. He said I should have thought about that before I disobeyed him. I stare at the barn, lit up with lanterns at every window. I long to be inside, smelling wood, hearing the hammer's song.

Why can't Papa see I only want to help?

At first I am determined to pay no attention to Christmas. Confined to the house and treated like a baby, I want to ignore William's excitement, Mama's menu planning and decorating. But the wonder of the season works its spell on me and brightens my mood.

I try another cookie recipe for ginger snaps. This time I make the dough into a log and slice it into perfect circles. Once they're baked to crispy perfection, I let everyone eat one, then divide the rest into Mama's tins so there will still be some left during the holiday.

I help Mama hang greenery on the door and in the windows of the dining room and parlor. The evergreen fragrance is almost as satisfying as the carriage barn smells.

Almost.

I tell Mama how much I want to finish the toy carriage for Papa. She must work some magic on him, because a week before Christmas, Sam brings the box of tools and model carriage to the house and tells me I can work on it here.

"How did you get Papa to change his mind?" I ask Mama.

"I simply reminded him you were making it to please him."

While I'd like to think that was all it took, I suspect Papa gave in because he has a hard time saying no to Mama. Either way, I am grateful for Mama's intervention on my behalf.

I put two coats of green paint all over the wooden base. Mama helps me cover the seat with a scrap of wool and glue it in place. Then I let Will dab bits of white paint all over the outside so it looks like snowballs. Henry sends over the finished iron frame and Mama and I nail it to the wood.

It comes out better than I imagined it would. Maybe because Mama and Will helped.

A few days before Christmas, Papa takes us on a sleigh ride over the snowy roads and countryside, so we can pick out the perfect tree. Watching William's excitement, running from tree to tree, reminds me that this is one of my favorite traditions. We all put the pretty glass ornaments on the tree Papa sets up in the parlor. Then Papa lifts William onto his shoulders so he can put the angel on the top. That's usually my job, but I decide to let William do it. It makes him feel big and important, and every time he looks up at that angel, his face glows and shines like the candles on the branches. He deserves to feel that special.

On Christmas Eve, Charlie and his sisters ask if William and I can go caroling. Mama surprises me by saying yes. We sing up and down the streets between our houses and end with cups of hot cider and spice cake in front of the warm fire at Charlie's house. Mrs. Cook has a basket of homemade goodies for me to bring home. I give her a tin of my cookies and a big jar of spiced peaches from Mama.

Charlie gives Will a bag of the prettiest colored marbles. He says he has so many, he won't miss them. He's polished them up so they look like new. I teach Will how to play with them and before the night is over, he is almost as good as me.

There is an unexpected surprise from Henry on Christmas Eve as well. It is a heart-shaped cookie cutter he made out of tin. It even has a handle to press into the dough. Now I can make twice as many cookies in half the time. I give Henry a big tin of my cookies to share with his family.

The next morning, I surprise Mama with a photograph of me and William that Mr. Cook took with his camera. Charlie helped me make a frame for it and we wrapped it in a red piece of scrap cloth and tied with a green ribbon from Mama's sewing box. Mama is so pleased, she sets it on the mantle over the fireplace.

I didn't feel right asking Mama for money to buy William a gift, so I made a little mouse from a discarded piece of leather from the barn. I stuffed it with some of Mama's fabric scraps. Mama showed me how to do some fancy stitching. I worked on it a long time, being stuck in the house and all.

My stitches are uneven and clumsy. But you can still tell it's a mouse and Will makes a big fuss over it.

"I'm calling him Mousie Two," he says, hugging it tightly. "He can sleep with me, right?" he asks Mama.

"Yes, he can," Mama says.

Mama smiles at me in a way that lets me know she is pleased with the gift.

Mama gives me a new nightgown, stockings, and boots. Papa's gift is a book called Tom Sawyer by his favorite author, Mark Twain. Mama thinks a more appropriate book would be A Young Girl's Guide to Etiquette. It thrills me that Papa knows I'd enjoy the antics of Tom Sawyer more than Mama's choice.

I also get some piano sheet music called "Maple Leaf Rag" by Scott Joplin.

Mama says, "I bought that before you stopped your lessons. It's one of my favorites. Maybe you'll be able to play it one day."

And who knows, maybe I will. I give Mama a big hug and thank her.

I've been saving the best for last. After Will gives Papa the picture he drew of a carriage — one that looks suspiciously like a Model T — I hand him my carefully wrapped package. As I watch Papa open it, his eyes light up brighter than the candles on the tree.

"You did this yourself?" Papa asks, holding up the model carriage. I can tell he's proud by the way he looks at me.

"With Mama and Will," I say.

"We hardly did anything," Mama corrects.

"The workmanship is really fine." Papa runs his hands

over the framework. "If you were a boy, you'd make a great apprentice to Sam."

Knowing Papa appreciates the work takes some of the sting out of those words. I wonder if now he'll let me back into the barn. Does he see how much I belong there?

Christmas is so pleasant, it makes me forget things are not going well for Papa's business. I get an awful reminder when I tiptoe downstairs two days after Christmas and overhear Mama and Papa talking in the kitchen.

"I don't know what I'm going to do when this job is over." There's worry in Papa's voice. "There are no more orders for carriages."

"Maybe you could find something at one of the businesses in town," Mama suggests.

"Doing what, Ella?" I hear anger and worry in his voice. "Making carriages is all I know."

"We've managed before. You'll think of something. We'll be all right, John."

Mama's words are meant to be encouraging, but Papa must hear the worry behind them, same as I do.

A week later the barn is locked and dark. No one comes or goes.

Tired of pretending nothing is wrong, I ask Mama why.

She sighs. "Papa's looking for work."

"What kind of work?"

"I don't know, Emily."

"Is the barn going to be closed forever?" My insides freeze up at the thought of no more magic coming from its walls.

Mama's sigh is so heavy it makes her shrink when it's done. "We'll have to wait and see," she says.

I curl up onto the settee, between Mama and Will. We sit like that awhile, quiet and wondering.

And maybe a little scared too.

CHAPTER 29

Turns out I'm not good at waiting and seeing. I decide to write a letter. I don't know if it will help, but it makes me feel better to do something. Surely it can't hurt.

January 3,1909

Dear Mr. Roosevelt Sir,

My papa, John Soper, made a beautiful carriage for you. It took him many hours of hard work to make the best carriage he could. Why didn't you greet him and say thank you? Papa says work is its own reward, but Mama says it's good manners to thank someone for doing a job, no matter how small.

If I were president, I would try to remember that just because I have an important job, it doesn't mean I'm the most important person. Papa takes real good care of our family and the people who work for him.

To me, that's the most important job of all.

I know you appreciate hard work, which was why I was so disappointed you weren't present to accept Papa's carriage. Some folks say that you are a friend of small businesses like the Soper Carriage Works. If that's true, since you know a lot of important people, I'll bet some of them would love a carriage like the one Papa made for you. I am hoping you could tell some of your friends about Papa. He could use new customers to keep the business going.

If you can help in any way, I'd be forever grateful. The work that goes on in Papa's barn is magical. Papa would be lost without that work. Wouldn't you be lost without yours?

Sincerely,

Emily Soper, age 12

When Sam picks me up from school, I ask if we can stop and mail the letter. I hand him the envelope and two pennies for a stamp. I got the pennies from Mama's emergency can. I figure this is an emergency.

"You can stick it in the mailbox, and when the mailman comes by, he'll pick it up," Sam says.

"I don't want Papa to see it."

Sam stops walking and says, "Emily, if you have a letter that will upset your daddy, I don't want to be any part of it. Seems to me if you're trying to get back in your daddy's good graces, you're going about it the wrong way."

"I'm trying to help you, Henry, and Papa," I say. Sam doesn't seem convinced.

There's only one thing left to do. I tell him about the letter's contents, hoping he will see my side.

Sam is quiet a minute, rubbing his chin with a hand

stained brown from so much varnish. "Well," he says. "I don't figure a letter like that is going to do your daddy or any of us much good. And complaining to Mr. Roosevelt about his behavior is disrespectful."

"I wasn't trying to be disrespectful," I insist. "I thought if Mr. Roosevelt knew all the work that went into the carriage, he might be able to help Papa. Mr. Roosevelt knows a lot of people and maybe some of them might need a carriage."

"I suppose things couldn't get much worse with the barn already closed," Sam says. "You tell Mr. Roosevelt you mean no disrespect, and we'll mail the letter. I don't think it'll do any harm."

"Thanks, Sam."

I sure hope it will do some good.

Chapter 30

On Saturday, Charlie and I finally get a chance to be together without Sam hovering over me. We're kicking up stones and looking for odd-shaped ones. I find one that looks like a heart and slip it into the pocket of my coat.

"I need to talk to your papa," Charlie says, bending to pick up his own stone.

"What for?" I ask.

"Daddy's hay wagon needs to be fixed. The place we got it from went out of business, and Daddy was wondering . . ."

"Sure he can!" I nearly jump out of my skin I'm so excited.

"How'd you know what I was going to ask?" Charlie smiles, pocketing the stone.

"You want Papa to fix the wagon."

"Can he?"

I stand, hands on hips. "Charlie Cook, you know he

can." I run the rest of the way home, leaving Charlie to catch up. I burst through the kitchen door, rattling the windows and feeling brighter than a sparkler on Independence Day.

"What on earth?" Mama frowns at my noisy entrance.

"Where's Papa?"

"Emily Soper, that is not the proper way to enter this house."

"I know, Mama, but I have a job and an idea for Papa and I want to tell him right away!"

"What do you mean you have a job? What are you talking about?" Mama looks past me at Charlie, who's finally caught up and stands in the open doorway.

"Land sakes alive!" Mama says. "Shut the door before the heat gets out."

I do as Mama asks. She puts down her rolling pin, and Charlie tells her about the broken wagon.

"Your father said he was going to the barn to do some work. Check there."

Papa's coming out of the barn as we get there. After Charlie tells him about the wagon, Papa sighs. "There's not much to fixing a wagon. Tell your daddy to bring it over."

As Charlie runs home, I run to the barn to tell Papa my idea. The one that has me snapping and sparking inside.

I take Papa's hand. "I know folks who buy your carriages can afford motorcars too, Papa. I also know you're worried about not having work. I have a new idea."

"What is your new idea?"

"All this time, we liked everything to be just as it is. But some changes can bring really good things, Papa. Like colored folks living peacefully next to white folks, and women getting to vote. What if you changed carriage making into something else?"

"Like what?"

"Maybe folks still need other things that horses pull. Wagons, carts, surreys, and coaches." My eyes open wider as more ideas pop into my head. "Baby buggies will never need motors. Sleighs and sleds for winter . . ."

"Emily," Papa stops me. "Where did you get this idea?"

"When Charlie mentioned fixing Mr. Cook's wagon because the man they bought it from went out of business, I thought there might be room for a new business. If you just change things a little bit . . ."

Seems like I've been expecting everybody around me to change, when I kept on telling myself things have to be just like they are. How crazy is that? If I'm expecting Mama, Papa, Mrs. Peabody, and everyone else to change their ways of thinking and doing things, I ought to practice what I preach.

Now I'm ready to change my ways.

If only I can convince Papa.

It's hard to figure out what Papa's thinking until his eyes rest on me. He's appeared tired and defeated since the fire. Now there's a new spark in his eyes as he smiles his quiet smile and says, "Not only did you save this barn, you saved your papa."

"How did I do that?"

"By opening my eyes to possibilities. I've been so fixed on preserving the old way of life, I let it get in the way of clear thinking. Instead of cursing change and progress, I should have been finding a way to be part of it."

Papa looks at me and says, "Your idea is perspicacious."

"Perspa what?" I ask, and Papa smiles. I am so happy to hear a new word — even one I can't pronounce.

"Perspicacious means thoughtful, intelligent, and clearheaded."

"It is very perspicacious of you to recognize my abilities," I say.

Papa's laughter thrills me to my toes. I dance circles around him on the way back to the house, reciting my new word like a song.

When we get back to the house, there's a bicycle on the grass, leaning against the wall. Mama and Claudia — I mean Miss Porter — greet us at the door.

"There you are, Emily. Just the girl I've been looking for," Claudia greets me, eyelids flapping like the wings of a hummingbird. "I've been concerned that you haven't returned for piano lessons, especially since you're my star pupil."

I don't think it's proper for me to tell her about Papa's money problems, so I look at Mama, then Papa, wondering what to say.

Papa looks at Mama and nods.

Mama says, "I explained to Claudia at church last Sunday that we are having some financial difficulties, which we hope will be temporary."

"Oh." I'm relieved I don't have to lie.

"That's why I'm here," Claudia says. "How would you like to be my apprentice? You can teach the young pupils the basic piano lessons in exchange for your own lessons when we're done." She looks at me with eyes wide open, as if her lids are glued that way. For the first time, I see her beautiful golden-brown eyes, like sunshine on an autumn day.

"You mean it?"

She nods and her eyelids go back to their frantic flapping.

"That will be grand," I tell her.

We make plans to begin after school on Monday. When we've all said our good-byes, Mama looks at me and asks, "Wasn't that a lovely surprise?" Her smile is sneaky.

"You already knew about this, didn't you?"

Mama and Papa look at each other, then at me, and both nod.

"And you didn't say anything?" Looks like I'm not the only one with secrets.

"Wasn't it more special hearing it from Claudia?" Mama asks.

"It was a wonderful surprise," I admit.

"Well, prepare yourself for another one."

"What do you mean?"

Mama hands me a letter. "Why would the president write to you?"

"Um . . . I wrote to him," I mumble. I know my face is red. Is it possible to be nervous, embarrassed, ashamed, and excited all at the same time?

Mama shakes her head like she can't believe I'm her daughter. Then she looks at Papa, who shrugs his shoulders and sighs. "I'm just about done in from all these surprises," he says. Underneath it, there is a sparkle in his eyes.

I stare at the letter. It's the first letter I've ever gotten in my entire life. The ivory-colored paper is thick with tiny threads and fibers in it like cloth. I can smell the ink from the fountain pen used to write my name in a lovely flowing script. I know Miss Carlisle would give the writer an A for beautiful penmanship.

"Read it," Papa urges, handing me his letter opener. The sparkle has won the day and a smile teases the corners of his mouth.

I slice through the top of the envelope, my hands shaking. "It's an invitation from Mr. Roosevelt," I say.

The President and Mrs. Roosevelt
request the pleasure of the company of
Miss Soper
at a reception to be held at
The White House
Thursday evening, February the fourth
nineteen hundred and nine
from nine to half after ten o'clock

I hold my breath tight. Will Papa let me have such a night? "You can't go alone," he says.

It hurts my heart. How perspicacious do I have to be for Papa to trust me?

"Does Sam have to bring me?" I ask.

"No. But I do. The president would not expect you to be unescorted."

I throw my arms around Papa and hug him tight. Having him with me will make it a perfect night.

CHAPTER 31

I think about the invitation all week. I know it's not polite to boast, but if I don't tell someone, I might explode like a firecracker. Who better to tell than Charlie? I swear him to secrecy, and since Beatrice isn't around to eavesdrop, the secret's safe. Charlie gives me his prized 1897 Indian Head penny — from the year we were born — to take along for luck, so I can tell he's excited for me.

Mama has me wear my best velvet dress. She waves to us as Papa helps me into the carriage for our evening ride to the White House.

On the way, my stomach is a tornado of what-ifs. What if the president didn't like Papa's carriage? What if the president doesn't like me? What if I embarrass myself with improper behavior? I should have paid more attention to Mama's instructions. I loosen my hold on the tin of cookies I made for President Roosevelt when I notice my fingers turning white, just like that time riding with Archie.

We're escorted into the East Room of the White House. Papa said Mr. Roosevelt had the room added on so he could have a grand place to entertain and play with his children. The newspaper said this is where they roller skated! The room is so enormous, I'll bet our whole house could fit inside. It has a polished wood floor in a fancy pattern that Papa calls parquetry. Upholstered benches line the walls between door-sized windows. Besides bronze electric lights mounted on the walls, there are three cut-glass chandeliers on the high ceiling that sparkle like diamonds. The walls are paneled in wood and painted white. There's even a portrait of George Washington hanging on one wall. I'll bet a queen's palace wouldn't look any grander.

So many people smiling, eating, and drinking. Everyone is wearing their Sunday best, so I'm glad Mama made me wear my new dress. The room hums with excited murmurs and whispers. I don't see anyone else my age. Some of the ladies look at me as if I might have wandered into the wrong place. I hold Papa's hand tighter as folks form a horseshoe around the room. A sudden hush makes me look toward the entrance.

The President and Mrs. Roosevelt enter.

They smile and greet each person as if they've known them all their lives. Mrs. Roosevelt has a lovely smile that makes you feel welcome. She sure seems right at home in this huge place. I can't help but wonder how she feels about women's suffrage and all the changes taking place.

Tonight, though, I am here for Papa.

When the president gets to me, his smile widens and he says in a commanding voice, "Are you Miss Soper, the proud daughter of the craftsman who made my beautiful carriage?"

"I am . . . sir." The words come out squeaky, so I take a deep breath to calm my nervousness. His blue eyes are so intense, my legs get wobbly, and I have to look at his mustache to keep from shaking.

"I am very pleased to meet you." He shakes my hand so hard, if I were a pump, water would gush onto the floor. "Mrs. Roosevelt and I spend many pleasant afternoons riding in your papa's carriage." Mr. Roosevelt smiles at Papa. "A friend is looking to buy a quality carriage. I gave him your name."

"Thank you, sir." They shake hands. Papa's face glows from the compliment. It surprises me that Mr. Roosevelt is only a couple of inches taller than Papa's five foot six. He seems like a giant in the newspapers.

"Your daughter's letter reminded me of the importance of honoring a job well done."

Papa says, "Emily mentioned a letter. Perhaps she should apologize."

"Not at all!" The president waves his hand dismissively. "You can't fault her for being proud of you."

Papa puts a hand on my shoulder and looks at me as if he's found a treasure. Standing here with him like this is even better than being in the carriage barn.

I almost forget until the weight in my hand reminds me to give Mr. Roosevelt the cookies I brought. I nearly drop the tin as I hand it to him.

"What do we have here?" he asks.

I take a deep breath and blurt out, "I made some sugar cookies because I thought you would like them and maybe Archie would too." It comes out so fast, it sounds like one long word. I sigh in embarrassment.

"You know the way to my heart, young lady." His eyes twinkle as he pats his stomach. "Thank you kindly, Miss Soper. Did you enjoy your ride with Archie?"

"It was grand," I say in a nearly normal voice. But the question makes the heat rise in my face.

"Is there something you haven't told me?" Papa's eyes are wide with curiosity.

"I'll explain later," I murmur.

"I think you'll have a lot of explaining to do." Mr. Roosevelt chuckles. His pince-nez glasses wiggle on his nose. I love how his whole face laughs along with him. He invites us to enjoy the refreshments and moves on to greet the next guest.

When the evening is over and Papa helps me into my coat, he asks, "Emily, what made you write to the president?"

"I couldn't bear the thought of the barn closing. I figured since Mr. Roosevelt is good at fixing things that are important, he might be able to fix that. The barn and what goes on there is magic, Papa."

Papa kisses my cheek. "You are a daughter to be proud of. As for the barn closing, that was temporary. I'll have to make a few changes inside the building. Mr. Coopersmith, the banker who holds our mortgage, has approved a small-business loan to help that get started. You remember Mrs. Coopersmith from the Tea?"

I nod, pleased to hear that she didn't believe Mrs. Peabody's claim of Papa's poor-quality work.

"And thanks to someone's excellent suggestion, I'll be making wagons, carts, baby buggies, and sleds. I've been asking around town, and there's plenty of need for a business like that. Sam and Henry are excited about the new products and anxious to get started." Papa's brow still has those worry crinkles.

"What about you, Papa? Aren't you excited?"

"I am. But to tell you the truth, I'm a bit anxious as well."

I take hold of Papa's hand. "Me too. Not knowing what's to come is scary. But all of us — you, me, Mama, Will, Henry, Sam — can face the changes together. That will make it easier than doing it alone, don't you think?"

Papa smiles, shakes his head, and plants a kiss on my forehead.

"What?" I ask.

"Sometimes I find it hard to believe that you're my daughter." His happy smile is a wonderful sight. "I suppose you could help sort nails, nuts and bolts, and the like. And I could use a hand with keeping the office space tidy."

"But what about being a proper lady?" I ask, my heart dancing.

Papa winks. "I won't tell Mama if you won't."

"Actually, some of the things Mama wanted me to learn have come in handy. I love to bake. People seem to like my cookies enough that maybe they would even buy them."

"They might at that. I'm sure your mama will be pleased to hear that. Just as I'm going to enjoy hearing all about your adventure with Archie Roosevelt."

Papa is smiling even bigger now.

"Maybe Henry and Sam ought to hear the story too," I say.

"Why don't you come to the barn tomorrow after school. We can all enjoy it then."

Now that's music to my ears.

Author's Note

The setting and final event of *Wheels of Change* is based on family history. My paternal great-grandfather (William Soper) worked as a carriage maker in Washington, DC, at the turn of the twentieth century. He worked on carriages for John Phillip Sousa and other prominent people. My grandmother — the original Mary Emily — was invited to a reception given by President Roosevelt at the White House. The invitation in the story is a copy of the original one that is in our family scrapbook. Based on National Archive records, Mary Emily attended the reception with her mother, Mrs. William Soper. While I haven't been able to locate the exact kind of carriage William worked on, the Brougham model in the story was ordered by Teddy Roosevelt while he was at the White House in 1902. It is now on display at the Henry Ford Museum in Dearborn, Michigan. The maker of the carriage is unknown.

I changed a few family facts in order to have a more child-oriented story. The age of my grandmother at the time of the reception was eighteen, rather than twelve. She also had six siblings. I gave her one to simplify the storytelling. All the other characters exist only in my imagination. The descriptions of DC, a carriage barn, the White House stables, the Brougham Carriage, and the East Room of the White House are taken from photos and historical documents. The rest of *Wheels of Change* is a work of fiction. Any mistakes or inaccuracies are strictly my own.

My grandmother grew up to become a piano player for silent movie houses in the DC area until she got married and had a family.

The President and Mrs. Roosevelt

request the pleasure of the company of

Miss Soper

at a reception to be held at

The White House

Thursday evening, February the fourth

nineteen hundred and nine

from nine to half after ten o'clock

Mary Emily Soper

MAMA'S PEACH PIE

For one, 2-crust 9-inch pie

Crust:
- 1 1/2 cups flour
- 1/4 teaspoon salt
- 1/2 cup shortening (see note)
- 3 to 4 tablespoons cold water.

1. Cut shortening into flour and salt until it's the texture of oatmeal.
2. Add water — one tablespoon at a time until dough forms. Dough should be dry to the touch.
3. Divide dough into two portions.
4. Lightly roll out one piece of dough onto a floured surface until it is the size of the pie pan.
5. Set it into the pan and fill it up with fruit mixture. Roll out remaining dough and cover the fruit.
6. Crimp the edges to seal it.

Filling:
1. Peel and slice enough peaches for five cups of fruit.
2. Sprinkle with 1/4 cup of sugar and 1 teaspoon of cinnamon.
3. Add 1 tablespoon of flour and stir until peaches are coated.
4. Pour into prepared crust. Add a few dots of butter to the peaches.
5. Seal with top crust, as noted above.
6. Bake in a hot oven (450 degrees) for 15 minutes, then reduce heat to 350 for 30 to 40 minutes or until crust is golden and peaches are tender.

Note: Emily's mama used lard instead of shortening. Lard is animal fat and is not used very much by today's cooks.

Mrs. Jackson's Gingerbread

- 1/4 pound butter or shortening
- 2 1/2 cups flour
- 1 cup sugar
- 2 teaspoons baking soda
- 1/2 teaspoon salt
- 2 teaspoons ginger
- 2 eggs
- 3/4 cup boiling water
- 3/4 cup molasses
- 1 tablespoon white vinegar

1. Set oven to 350 degrees.
2. Grease and flour a square cake pan.
3. Cream butter and sugar in a large bowl. Add eggs. Add water, molasses, and vinegar. Stir until blended.
4. Add dry ingredients to wet mixture. Pour into prepared pan.
5. Bake 35 to 45 minutes. If a toothpick inserted in the center of the cake comes out dry, it's done.

EMILY'S BISCUITS

- •2 cups flour
- •1 tablespoon sugar
- •1/2 teaspoon salt
- •4 tablespoons baking powder
- •1/2 cup shortening
- •2/3 cup milk

1. Set oven to 425 degrees.
2. Cut shortening into dry ingredients until mixture resembles coarse crumbs.
3. Add milk all at once.
4. Knead fourteen times.
5. Pat dough to ½-inch thickness. Cut in rounds using a glass turned upside down. CUT STRAIGHT DOWN. DO NOT TWIST.
6. Place 1 inch apart on a cookie sheet. Bake for 15 to 20 minutes or until golden brown.

EMILY'S SUGAR COOKIES

- 1/4 pound butter
- 3/4 cup sugar
- 1 egg
- 1/2 teaspoon vanilla
- 1 tablespoon cream or milk
- 1 1/4 cups flour
- 1/8 teaspoon salt
- 1/4 teaspoon baking powder

1. Set oven to 350 degrees.
2. Cream the butter, then gradually add the sugar, beating until light.
3. Add the egg, vanilla, and cream or milk, and beat thoroughly.
4. Mix the flour, salt, and baking powder together, add to the first mixture, and blend well.
5. Arrange by teaspoonfuls on cookie sheets, 1 inch apart.
6. Bake for 8 to 10 minutes or until lightly browned.

Note: Recipes were adapted from the 1896 edition of the Fannie Farmer Cookbook *and the* Boston Cooking-School Cook Book.

ACKNOWLEDGMENTS

There are so many people who assisted in so many ways to bring this book to life.

A talented and dedicated group of children's book writers critiqued early drafts of *Wheels of Change* when I envisioned it as a picture book. Theresa Wallace Pregent, Narcissa Smith-Harris, Francesca Amendolia, Bette Lynn McIlvaine and Michele Lacina made me think there might be a story worth telling. Thanks for your tough love on those early drafts.

Eve Adler, editor at Grosset and Dunlap, provided detailed feedback on that early picture book version and suggested I expand the story into a middle-grade novel. I am forever grateful for that encouragement and foresight.

A second critique group I met at the New Jersey SCBWI conference read numerous drafts of the middle-grade version, providing detailed comments and suggestions. My deepest appreciation to these wonderful and talented women: Sandra Hartnett, Lynda Gene Rymond, Jean Trujillo, and Mary Zisk. Your care and commitment to detail helped me fine-tune Emily's voice. Many thanks to the other members of NJSCBWI for all the warm fuzzies and positive vibes you always send whenever we're together.

Many thanks to Editor Christy Ottaviano of Christy Ottaviano Books for her enthusiasm and some great editorial advice/guidance in the early stages of the manuscript.

Special thanks to my former writer's group and friends from Pen-In-Hand for listening to chapters and providing encouragement. You guys are awesome.

I am indebted to the following people for answering countless questions about Washington, DC, carriage making, and American culture at the turn of the twentieth century.

Bronwen Sanders was my carriage expert from the Mifflinburg Buggy Museum in Mifflinburg, PA. She, along with the museum, provided a wealth of information on the workings and operation of a turn-of-the-century carriage factory, and gave me the perfect setting for the story. This museum is a treasure and the only original historical carriage factory in existence in the United States. See www.buggymuseum.org

Mark Koziol, the museum tech for the National Park Service at Sagamore Hill (Teddy Roosevelt's home on Long Island), answered questions about Teddy Roosevelt.

The Historical Society of Washington, DC, and Steve Davenport, the reference librarian at the Library of Congress provided information about the nation's capital in the early 1900s. They also recommended books and maps of the era that helped paint a picture of the time period.

Carol Ann Missant from the Henry Ford Museum in Dearborn, Michigan, sent a picture of the Brougham carriage belonging to Teddy Roosevelt that is on permanent display at the museum. She also sent detailed descriptions of the materials used in its construction. These details added depth and richness to the carriage-making sections of the book. See www.thehenryford.org

I extend a special appreciation to the White House Historical Association for answering many questions regarding Teddy Roosevelt's tenure in the White House. They graciously provided a photo of the stables on Seventeenth Street (which once stood across from the current Corcoran Gallery of Art). Their expertise regarding DC life in the early 1900s was invaluable and brought the era to life for me.

I also wish to thank my friend Kathy Temean. Besides being a wonderful resource on all things regarding writing for children, she's a talented illustrator, web designer, and conference organizer. It was through her introduction that I met and pitched *Wheels of Change* to agents Liza Fleissig and Ginger Harris of the Liza Royce Agency.

These super agents and remarkable women believed in this book from the beginning and worked tirelessly finding a home for it. Their over-the-top love, support, and enthusiasm for *Wheels of Change* still amazes me. You women make me proud to be a writer of children's books.

This book would not exist if Marissa Moss — children's book author and editor and publisher at Creston Books — weren't willing to take a chance on an unknown writer. Her editorial style, plot suggestions, and attention to detail made *Wheels of Change* bigger and better than I could have imagined. Her insight is extraordinary.

Finally, my deepest love, gratitude and appreciation to all my friends for their continuing support, and my family — past and present — for loving me, encouraging me, and inspiring me. Thank you all from the bottom of my heart.

BIBLIOGRAPHY

Bundy, Beverly. *The Century in Food: America's Fads and Favorites.* Collector's Press, 2002. Pages 6—27.

Coleman, Penny. *Girls: A History of Growing up Female in America.* Scholastic, 2000.

Collins, Herbert Ridgeway. *Presidents on Wheels.* Washington, DC: Acropolis Books, 1971.

Epstein, Dan. *20th Century Pop Culture.* Carlton Books, 1999. Pages 6—8.

Goode, James M. *Washington Sculpture.* The Johns Hopkins University Press, 2008.

Hakim, Joy. *Age of Extremes.* Oxford University Press, 1994.

Passonneau, Joseph R. *Washington Through Two Centuries.* The Monacelli Press, 2004.

Roosevelt, Theodore. *Letters and Speeches.* The Library of America, 2004.

Rosenberger, Jim. *America 1908.* Scribner and Sons, 2007.

Whitcomb, John and Claire. *Real Life at the White House: 200 Years of Daily Life at America's Most Famous Residence.* Rutledge Publishing, 2000. Pages 219—235.

WEB RESOURCES

For more information about *Wheels of Change*, including curriculum guides, visit the Teacher page at crestonbooks.co.

streetsofwashington.com is a valuable resource for details regarding commercial establishments along Seventh Street and the surrounding areas at the turn of the twentieth century.

theodore-roosevelt.com/trfamily.html provides photos and short videos of Roosevelt and his family.

ABOUT THE AUTHOR

Darlene Beck Jacobson has a BA in Special Education and a Reading Specialist MA. She worked as a Speech Language Specialist with the Glassboro Public Schools in Glassboro, NJ for 20 years. When not writing books, she substitute-teaches for Pre-K and K classes in her former school district.

Beck Jacobson has loved writing since she was a girl. She wrote letters to everyone she knew and made up stories in her head. Although she never wrote to a president, she sent many letters to pop stars of the day asking for photos and autographs.

Her stories have appeared in *Cicada, Cricket,* and other magazines. Her blog features recipes, activities, crafts and interviews with children's book authors and illustrators. For more information about Darlene, visit her at darlenebeckjacobson.com.